A Gangster's Syn 2

Lock Down Publications and
Ca$h Presents

A Gangster's Syn 2

A Novel by **J-Blunt**

A Gangster's Syn 2

Lock Down Publications
P.O. Box 870494
Mesquite, Tx 75187

Visit our website
www.lockdownpublications.com

Lock Down Publications
Like our page on Facebook: Lock Down Publications @
www.facebook.com/lockdownpublications.ldp
Cover design and layout by: **Dynasty Cover Me**
Book interior design by: **Shawn Walker**
Edited by: **Lauren Burton**

Stay Connected with Us!

Text **LOCKDOWN** to 22828 to stay up-to-date with new releases, sneak peeks, contests and more...

Submission Guideline.

Submit the first three chapters of your completed manuscript to ldpsubmissions@gmail.com, subject line: Your book's title. The manuscript must be in a .doc file and sent as an attachment. The document should be in Times New Roman, double-spaced and in size 12 font. Also, provide your synopsis and full contact information. If sending multiple submissions, they must each be in a separate email.

Have a story but no way to send it electronically? You can still submit to LDP/Ca$h Presents. Send in the first three chapters, written or typed, of your completed manuscript to:

LDP: Submissions Dept
Po Box 870494
Mesquite, Tx 75187

DO NOT send original manuscript. Must be a duplicate.

Provide your synopsis and a cover letter containing your full contact information.

Thanks for considering LDP and Ca$h Presents.

A Gangster's Syn 2

Chapter 1

Loretta

"Did you see how Vega had Claire ass stuttering like she was talkin' to the police? 'I-I-I didn't know Sheba was yo' bitch,'" Jayda mocked.

We both burst out laughing. "But that is so wrong. Vega be on that bully shit. That ain't cool. She already know nobody won't fight her. Now she going around takin' people girlfriends. She gon' start takin' pussy next," I said as I closed our cell door behind us.

"She already did that. I'm surprised she hasn't tried you yet. Er'body know her big, black ass like redbones. You should probably get you a girl. I know Rain is diggin' you. And you know Vega won't fuck wit' Rain or her girls."

I eyed Jayda's back as she climbed onto the top bunk. She had been my cellmate for almost two years. She was doing a nine-year bid for robbery. Jayda was cool, and I trusted her enough to befriend her, but not enough to confide in her. I seen too many character flaws, mainly that she could be walked on, manipulated, or bullied. And the fact she was advising me to give my pussy away for protection against Vega was another notch on her character flaw tally.

"Girl, please. You know I ain't wit' that lesbian shit. I have hands. I know how to get myself off."

Jayda looked down at me like I had 'fool' written across my forehead. "Loretta, they gave you twenty-five years. You mean to tell me you gon' finger yo'self for the next quarter century instead of lettin' one of these good pussy-lickin' bitches suck yo' pussy?"

"That's exactly what I'm sayin'. I don't have to compromise myself because I'm in prison. That's the problem. Bitches is folding under pressure. Don't know how to stand up."

"Yeah, okay, Sistah Souljah. You been readin' too many of them Angela Davis books. They ass ain't doin' this time. You is.

7

And ain't neither one of them gon' be here to save yo' ass if Vega decide she want you to be her bitch."

"Have you lost yo' mind, Jayda? Ain't nobody takin' my pussy, bitch. What's wrong with you? You need to read more Angela Davis and Sistah Souljah books so you can develop a spine and not feel like you have to fuck with another girl for protection."

Jayda's face reflected anger and hurt. "Fuck you and the high horse you rode in on, Loretta," she spat before turning on her radio and putting on her headphones.

This was why I hated being locked up with women: too many damn emotions.

I was being housed at Taycheeda Correctional Institution, Wisconsin's maximum, medium, and minimum security prison for women. This had been my home for the past five years, and according to the judge I had twenty more to go unless I got parole. I wouldn't be eligible for that for another twelve years. All of this for killing the man who tried to rape me.

After giving Jayda one last salty look, I sat on my bed and grabbed the book that was lying on my pillow, Sistah Souljah's *No Disrespect*. This was one of my favorite books of all time. I liked what Sistah Souljah represented. A strong black woman with a true sense of self who stood up for what she believed in. She embodied everything I wanted to be: a powerful woman who could mentally whoop men and women. So, while I did my time, I planned to keep my face in books and search the depths of who I was to find my strengths. I planned to use my prison experience as a training ground so whenever they decided to let me go, I would be mentally tough and as focused as ever.

***

"I think women really run the world. Men have all the power, sure. But behind the scene, there is always a woman controlling that man," Sheena lectured to the seven women who were seated around the table.

We were in the library. All the women were seated at a table next to me. I was skimming through Carter G. Woodson's *Mis-Education of the Negro* and eavesdropping.

"See, back in the day, women leaned on a man for everything. He controlled the purse, so he had all of the power in the relationship. Whatever the man said was law. We couldn't argue with our provider. Nor could we vote. But somewhere along the way, women wised up. Not only did we fight and win our right to cast a ballot, but we also discovered the subtle power of sex and our sensuality. Discovered that everything a man did, he did it for one thing."

Sheena paused, letting us all ponder on what that one thing could be. And since Sheena mastered the art of orating, she held her answer long enough for us to slide our butts to the edge of our seats.

"For pussy. They need it. Will kill for it. What we have between our legs is more than a sex object, ladies. It is a gold mine of endless treasure and shouldn't just be given away. We must use what we have to get ourselves ahead."

All the women around the table shook their heads in agreement. I even found myself acknowledging her words. They were the truth.

"Checkout in five minutes!" the inmate library clerk called, signaling the library period was almost over. I grabbed my books and headed to the checkout counter.

"Hey!" someone call as I strolled across the prison yard. I looked back and seen Sheena high-stepping in my direction.

"Yeah. What's up?"

"Slow up. Lemme holler at you."

I slowed enough for her catch up to me. Sheena was brown-skinned, about 5'5", and 130 pounds. She wore her hair in cornrows that hung past her shoulders. She wasn't a pretty girl, but she wasn't ugly, either.

"So, what did you think about my lecture?" she asked when she was abreast of me.

"What?" I asked, faking ignorance.

"I knew you were listening. Carter G. Woodson didn't keep you in that seat all that time. You could have joined our group. We welcome everybody."

"I'm not into groups or cliques. I ride solo."

"Solo in prison is not wise. The wolves prey on the sheep that ride solo. We have strength in numbers. It is not weak to need people. God created voids in us to need human interaction, to keep us from being all about 'me'."

"I've been here for five years, and I've seen how nasty us women can be toward people they claim to ride with. If that's what having friends is all about, I don't want any."

"What is your name?"

"Loretta."

"Well, listen, Loretta. A real sistah don't do that traitorous, backstabbing trickery you are speaking of. The real recognizes the real. There are fake women pretending to be real all around us. But you can tell a tree by the fruit it bears."

"I feel you. A little bit. I guess I just haven't ran into anyone real yet."

"Real recognizes real. My name is Sheena. I'm as real as they come."

"I know who you are. I've seen you around."

"Cool. Well, I gotta head over to the chapel to pick up some things. I want to extend you an invite to attend our next meeting in the library. We meet up on Thursday at 2:30. You can meet some more like-minded women. We have to be our sistah's keepers around here. Our survival depends on it."

"Okay. I'll come."

"Alright. See you then. And by the way, that is a really good book, but I would also encourage you to read anything by Ivan Van Sertima and Na'aim Akbar."

After parting ways with Sheena, I headed back to the cell block. I was lost in thought about meeting these 'like-minded' sistahs on Thursday when Vega appeared in front of me. I didn't know where she came from. All I knew was I looked away for a moment, then looked back again and she was there.

I was surprised I'd missed her, too. She embodied the lyrics of the rapper Notorious B.I.G.: "Black and ugly as ever." She stood about six feet and weighed at least 250 pounds. Her skin was tar black, her hair cut short with brushed waves, and she looked like a mix between Notorious B.I.G. and Godzilla. She looked just like an ugly-ass man. And a strong-ass one, too. She was the only chick on the compound who could bench press the entire 300 pound stack.

"'Sup, Loretta?" she smiled, chomping on her gum like it was the last piece on earth.

"Hey, Vega," I said, trying hard to act like I didn't notice the way she was looking me up and down. My prison greens weren't tight, but they fit me and showed off my figure in a way I couldn't help.

"Wait up one minute." She stepped in front of me, blocking my path and forcing me to stop. "When you gon' join a nigga team, ma? I been peepin' you for a minute, and I know you ain't fuckin' wit' nobody. Let me be that somebody."

"What? Nah, Vega. I don't get down like that. Strictly dickly," I said and attempted to walk around her.

As far as I was concerned, the conversation was over, but Vega didn't think so. She grabbed my arm to stop me from walking away. "Hold up."

I snatched away from her. "Don't touch me!" I said seriously. I didn't want any trouble, but I wasn't about to let her try me.

"Oh, shit! You's a feisty bitch. I love that. You ain't gon' be the first feisty bitch I fuck. I'm Vega. I get what I want," she said, giving me a sinister smile.

"Parson! Leave her alone and get moving!" a male guard called from behind us.

"I'ma get you, bitch!" Vega said menacingly before strolling away.

J-Blunt

Chapter 2

Two Months Later

"How do you feel about women having sex with other women?"

Sheena looked up from counting the eggs and gave me a suspicious leer. We were working as preparation cooks in the main kitchen. Our current task was to count out all the eggs for tomorrow's breakfast. I had gotten the job a month ago. I only made twenty-six cents an hour, but the time I got to spend with Sheena compensated for the lack of pay. She was one of the smartest women I had ever met. She believed in the encouragement and uplifting of women like I did, and she always had an intelligent opinion about social issues.

"Why are you asking me that? I didn't think you swung that way."

"I don't. I just want to know how you feel about it."

Sheena was quiet for a moment. "I don't know if you know this or not, Loretta, but I have a girlfriend."

The shocked look on my face let her know I was ignorant to her lesbian lifestyle.

"Chill, Loretta. It's not a big deal. Around here it's natural. I never talked to you about it because you made it clear on several occasions you didn't swing that way. If you noticed, whenever you spoke your opinion, I always remained silent."

I didn't know what to say. All I managed was a weak "Oh. Okay."

"Don't get me wrong, I love men. I like the muscles, the deep voice, the facial hair, their strength, and I love a big dick. But the truth is, I have life with no parole. I'm not ever getting out."

"Uh. Um. Okay."

Sheena put down the eggs she had in her hand and stared at me. "Loretta, stop. If there is something on your mind, say it."

I thought about what I wanted to say and how I should say it. The last thing I wanted to do was offend my friend. "I wanted to know how you felt about gay women. But now that I know you're gay, I don't need to know anymore."

Sheena gave me a look that let me know she knew I was holding back. "Every case is not the same, Loretta. Me personally, I don't like butches. I like fine women. Like you. And I'm not hitting on you, either, so don't be gettin' funny. I'm just saying you look good. And I said that because I don't want to replace men like some of these women. I like men and women. And believe me, as much as I loved my Brian, he could never please me like my girlfriend. Denise is a woman, and she knows what I want because she wants the same things."

"I just never imagined a world where this was normal. I can't see myself with a woman. We are needy and emotional. Men are hard and strong. I like hard and strong."

"A hungry person don't care what kind of silverware they eat with."

Her comment made me pause and reflect. "Damn. I guess I never thought about it like that."

"I was just like you, Loretta. I hung on to my Christian values for the longest time. Growing up, my mom took me and my brother to church every Sunday. I heard all the fire and brimstone messages about gay people and fornicators going to hell. I used to think gay people were different. Sick. Confused. I never thought about messing with a woman until I came to prison. Does all of this sound familiar?"

"Yeah. Sounds like me, except for the part about the brother. I'm an only child. But I heard the sermons about homosexuals and cheaters going to hell. My dad was pretty strict. Wouldn't even let me talk to boys on the phone until I was seventeen. I met C-Money when I was–"

"Hold on, Loretta! Why you stop? It sounded like it was just about to get juicy."

"Um. I don't know. I didn't really want to get too personal."

"What? Are you serious? C'mon, Loretta. You have to trust somebody. Everybody is not out to get you."

"I know. And I'm sorry. It's just, I don't know. I'm not used to talking about me or telling my story."

"Well, listen. If we gon' continue to work together, you have to let that guard down. I'm about reciprocity."

"Okay. I got you."

"Good. Now, like I was saying, I never thought about messing with women until I got here. And even after I got here, it still took me three years to actually have sex with a woman. I had never been in trouble with the law, so I didn't know how it was in here. I thought prison was how it is in the movies. But now that I've been in almost eleven years, I've discovered this prison lifestyle is a kind of sub-culture. This place is its own world with its own rules. And since I got life and will probably never lay with a man again, I'ma fall in line with the rules of the sub-culture we live in. This is our reality."

***

"Suck my nuts, Loretta, while Rhoda suck my dick," Rasheed said, rubbing himself as he lay back on the bed.

I didn't want to do it. His dick was long and black, and he had hairy balls. I had only sucked one pair of balls in my life, and I didn't like doing it then. Plus, I didn't like the thought of being so close to my friend's face.

"C'mon, girl," Rhoda encouraged when she seen my hesitation.

I reluctantly crawled between Rasheed's legs just as Rhoda began sucking him. I watched them for a few moments. It felt like I was in a porno. She was sucking him good, like she was really enjoying it. Seeing her so eager to please turned me on so much that I bent down and began sucking the hairy balls.

Rasheed wiggled and thrashed beneath us. When I felt his sack tighten, I moved and watched Rhoda drink his cum. She didn't miss a beat. Rasheed moaned and twisted up his face as she sucked him dry.

"Now, that's how you suck a dick," Rhoda grinned.

"Take notes, Loretta. Go 'head and give her a kiss," Rasheed said, placing his hands behind his head as he looked back and forth from me to Rhoda.

"No. I told y'all, I'm good," I protested. She had just drank his cum. I didn't want to taste that.

"C'mon, Loretta. Quit being a party pooper," Rhoda whined, giving me puppy dog eyes.

I did not want to kiss my friend. I had already told them no, but I also didn't want to mess up their evening. After all, they had been taking care of me and my baby since C-Money got locked up.

"Okay," I reluctantly agreed.

We met in the middle of the bed. Her huge breasts smothered mine as we came chest-to-chest. I closed my eyes as our lips met. Rhoda's lips were big and soft, and I could taste Rasheed's cum when she stuck her tongue in my mouth. I felt her hands roam over my body, eventually stopping between my thighs. She parted my lips and found my hot box.

It felt good, and when she lay me down and climbed on top of me, I didn't protest. She spun around and put her hairy bush in my face. She wanted 69 with me. I was hesitant, but when she started sucking my love button, I forgot I was doing something I was against.

"Loretta! You not gon' believe what just happened!"

My eyes shot open. "Huh? What?" I asked, wiping the drool from my mouth.

"Vega and Rain just got into a fight. Vega beat her ass!" Jayda yelled excitedly.

I blinked the sleep out of my eyes as I tried to digest what I had been told. "What? Vega beat up Rain? You serious?" I asked, pulling the sheet off as I sat up in bed. I was hot.

"Hell yeah! They..."

I looked up at Jayda to see why she stopped talking. She was staring at my chest. I looked down to see what had caught her attention. My t-shirt was soaked with sweat. It looked like I had

16

been in a wet t-shirt contest, and my nipples were poking through the wet cotton like scud missiles.

"Looks like you was dreaming good," she smiled.

I didn't know what to say. I was horny. I had been right on the verge of cumming when she woke me up, and now I wanted to cum. Really bad. I thought about what Sheena said. "A hungry person don't care what kind of silverware they eat with."

Without speaking, I got up and walked over to Jayda. When I was close enough, I stuck my tongue in her mouth and kissed her. She was surprised at first, but quickly got with the program. I palmed her ass as we made out.

We eventually ended up on my bed, her on top. I was ready for action and got tired of the foreplay. "Suck my pussy," I told her after breaking the kiss.

"Girl, what has gotten into you?" she asked, searching my face as she knelt over me.

I didn't want to talk. "Stop talking. You fucking up the mood," I told her, pushing her off of me and snatching off my shorts.

After we were both naked, Jayda crawled between my legs and gave me what I wanted. When her tongue found my clit, I thought I was going to explode. It had been years since I had my pussy ate, and Jayda's tongue felt damn good. And Sheena was right. Women knew exactly what women wanted.

Jayda sucked my clit until I came, and then used her tongue like a dildo and stuck it in and out of me until I came again. I hadn't cum that hard in a long time. When we switched positions, I did the exact same things to her that she did to me.

We spent the rest of the day in bed, exploring each other's bodies. After we had taken each other to the peak and beyond a few times, she lay nestled in my arms. As much as I liked her tongue between my legs, I did not like her cuddled up next to me. She was soft. I wanted hard. I decided this would be the last time I ever cuddled another woman.

"Where you goin'?" Jayda asked after I climbed out of her bed.

"To my bed."

"Why?" she whined.

"It's almost count. I don't want first shift to see me in your bed."

"Oh. Okay. Wake me up when they count."

"I got you."

It didn't take long for Jayda to fall to sleep, Unfortunately, sleep didn't come that easy for me. I couldn't stop thinking about sex with Jayda. I liked it way more than I thought I would. What I didn't like was thoughts on how Jayda would perceive our tryst. She had been in relationships around the prison before, and she got attached. Fast. I didn't want that. I wanted our thing to be casual. No strings attached. No titles. I wasn't sure how I was going to convey this to Jayda, but I would. Soon.

***

I was sitting on my bunk reading my book when the cell door opened. Jayda walked in. She had just gotten off work.

"What you reading?"

"*48 Laws of Power*," I mumbled.

Jayda sat next to me and grabbed my book. "Why don't you put that book down and let me show you the 48 Laws of Pussy Licking?"

I snatched my book away from her. "Not right now. Move." I liked her tongue, but I didn't want her to get clingy. I wanted to control when we had sex and how we did it. I wanted to make it clear I didn't want a girlfriend.

"Why you actin' like that? You wasn't doin' that last night."

I sat my book down and looked her in her eyes. "Jayda, don't be getting all emotional and shit. We not girlfriends. We cool and can still fuck around, but don't think that just because you ate my pussy you got rights to me."

Jayda's face twisted into an angry mask. "So, that's how you want it? Want to act all funny and shit?"

18

"I'm not actin' funny, Jayda. You are. I don't want a girl. You my home girl. I don't want to be in a relationship. I'm not lookin' for love. I just want my pussy licked every now and then."

"Pst. Whatever," Jayda mumbled before climbing onto her bunk.

I smiled as I picked up my book. Game on!

J-Blunt

A Gangster's Syn 2

Chapter 3

"I wanna be a Boss Bitch."

"Loretta, you are tripping. A Boss Bitch, huh?" Jayda said and burst out laughing.

I stared disgustedly at her as she rolled around on her bed. I didn't understand why she was laughing. I wasn't playing around.

"What exactly is a Boss Bitch, and where did you get this ideal?"

"It came to me about a month ago when I read *Boss Lady*. I came up with my own concept about what a Boss Bitch is. It's a mentality, really. You hear these rappers and hood dudes callin' theyself Boss Niggas all the time. You see how they carry theyself. They got clout. Confidence. A set of rules they play by. People around them look up to them and respect their slot. I want that. I want to call the shots. I want to play by my own rules."

Jayda looked at me like I was an alien. "Are you serious, Loretta?"

"Yes. Don't you want to be somebody? Have a name for yourself? Be the head bitch in charge?"

"I don't know. I just wanna go home. Do my time and stay out of trouble. I don't want the attention."

"But what about the power? You don't have to be the center of attention to have power and call the shots. I don't want to be just plain old Loretta no more. I'm ready to spread my wings and fly."

"It sounds like you are letting being locked up make you crazy. I remember when I first met you. You was a good girl, all shy an' shit. Now look at you. You are becoming a different person. A Boss Bitch," she smirked.

"That's the point, Jayda. We are supposed to grow and change. We are supposed to get stronger and smarter. I don't want to be helpless or vulnerable no more. I think if I would've had some independence instead of depending so much on C-Money, I probably wouldn't be in here. I could've had my own money. My own life. But I didn't. I was dependent on him. And when he left, I

21

had to depend on somebody else. A Boss Bitch don't depend on nobody but herself. We call our own shots."

"Girl, you trippin'. What the fuck you been drinkin'? Where is the weed? You holdin' out?"

I cut my eyes at Jayda. "I knew I shouldn't have talked to you about this shit. You not ready. You will always be a worker. I'ma be an owner," I said before plopping down on my bed.

"I'm sorry, Loretta. I didn't mean it like that. I was just playing."

I ignored her. Fuck her. She was too small-minded. She would never understand.

"So, that's how it is, Loretta? Silent treatment? I said I was sorry."

I searched her face as she stood before me. She looked sorry. I wanted to see how sorry she really was. A test.

"Whatever," I said, fanning my hand at her as I reached for my headphones and turned on my TV.

"Don't be like that, Loretta. I said I'm sorry. What do you want me to do?"

I was waiting to hear those words. "Show me how sorry you are."

A lusty look flashed in her eyes. I knew what she was thinking, but I was about to change the game.

"What do you want me to do?"

"Suck my feet." I knew I was pushing it with my request, but I had to see what I could make her do.

She just stared at me. I thought she might curse me out or try to fight me.

"Okay."

I couldn't believe my ears, couldn't believe she was actually going to suck my feet until she knelt in front of me, pulled off my sock, and stuck my big toe in her mouth. But she didn't stop there. She moved her lips up and down my big toe like she was giving a man head. And then she took all five toes in her mouth and did the same. My pussy got super wet. It felt better than I thought it would. And when she licked the bottom of my feet from heel to toe, I knew I had her. She would do anything I wanted her to do. And knowing I had that kind of power over her turned me on.

"Lay on the bed," I ordered.

She did as she was told. I stood and snatched off her sweat-pants and panties. The pink lips of her shaved pussy were shining with wetness. I sat on the bed and started fingering her. One finger at first. Then two. Then three.

"Mm, damn!" she moaned as she gyrated on my hand.

I stared at her face as I worked my fingers in and out of her. Her eyes were closed and her face was drawn up in an ugly mug. I bent down and flicked my tongue across her clit.

"Aw, shit, Loretta!"

Hearing her say my name was hot. It got me excited. No one had ever called my name during sex. "Say my name again."

"Ooh, Loretta!"

My confidence was peaking. I felt like talking shit. "You gon' cum for me, Jayda? Let me see this pink pussy cum."

"Mm-hmm. Yeah, Loretta. I'ma cum for you, baby."

I bent down and began sucking her pearl again while I fin-gered her. Jayda went wild.

"Oh, shit, Loretta. Mm, yeah! I'm 'bout to cum!"

"Call me a Boss Bitch."

"Oh yeah, Boss Bitch!"

"Who a Boss Bitch?"

"You a Boss Bitch, Loretta! You a Boss Bitch!"

***

"I like that Boss Lady thing, Loretta. I might have to start using that," Sheena said after taking a sip from her cup of apple juice. We were in the chow hall having breakfast. Grits and waffles.

"Boss Bitch," I corrected.

"Why you gotta use bitch? I like lady better," Malissa cut in. Malissa was a member of our real sistahs crew. She was dark-skinned, stood about 5', and was a little chubby.

"I like Boss Bitch. It sounds official, like how a man would call himself a Boss Nigga," Melody cut in. She was also a member of our crew. She was light-skinned, almost 6' tall, and kind of pretty.

"Yeah, you feel me!" I said, giving Melody a high five.

"'Bitch' is derogatory, like 'nigga'. I ain't a dog," Sheena quipped.

"We're empowering the word bitch. Taking the sting out of it. Now, when somebody calls us a bitch, we can be like, 'Nah, get that shit right. I'm a Boss Bitch!'"

"Hell yeah!" Melody agreed, giving me another high five.

Sheena shook her head and laughed at us. "Y'all are crazy."

"Hey, ladies," someone interrupted from behind.

I spun around and seen Sophia standing over my shoulder. She was a young Puerto-Rican girl who had come to a few of our groups. She was pretty with a slim, model-like figure and big breasts. She didn't talk much at the groups and seemed a bit naïve, but she was cool.

"Hey, Sophia," we greeted her.

"Are y'all still meeting in the library today?" she asked, smiling down at me.

"Yeah. Same bat time, same bat channel," Sheena answered.

"Okay. Bye, y'all," she said, giving me a lingering stare as she walked away.

I caught the look. It was flirty, like she was crushing on me. I looked around the table to see if anyone noticed it. They didn't. They had already jumped back to the discussion about Boss Bitches and Boss Ladies.

"Tell me more about this Boss Bitch, Loretta. How much thought have you put into this? What are the qualifications?" Sheena asked.

"A Boss Bitch is a go-getter, an independent woman who is capable of being an independent thinker. She don't need nobody to complete her or validate her. She is who she is because she knows who she is. A Boss Bitch is responsible for her own happiness. She acknowledges her desire for intimacy, but tames the desperation for a love or lust that can turn her into a fool or finger-pointer. She is in control of every aspect of her life. A Boss Bitch takes care of her people, is trustworthy, and instead of reacting emotionally, she uses wisdom during disputes. Her word is her bond, and she don't break it for nobody. A Boss Bitch does what she says she's gon' do – no ifs, ands, or buts about it. A Boss Bitch never gets jealous or intimidated by another woman. She knows her worth and knows how to play her position. A Boss Bitch don't do the gossip shit. She handles her problems with whoever she has the problem with. And most importantly, a Boss Bitch don't snitch."

Sheena, Malissa, and Melody began clapping.

"Damn, Loretta. That was some of the realest shit I ever heard. I need you to write that down for me," Melody said, looking at me like I had just preached *The Sermon on the Mount.*

"Yeah, Loretta. That was on point. I'm feeling it," Sheena nodded. "Bring whatever you have written on that to the library, and we'll introduce it to the rest of the girls to see what they think."

***

During our meeting in the library, Sophia kept sneaking peeks at me. I had caught her several times, and every time I caught her, she smiled and looked away. Then, five minutes later, she was all up in my grill again. I decided I was going to try to fuck her. She was pretty, but I wasn't attracted to her. Seeing a fine or naked woman didn't excite me; I got turned on from physical contact. But I had to admit, in the looks department, she was an upgrade from Jayda. Not that it mattered that much because Jayda wasn't my woman. She was a fuck buddy. And even though I wasn't attracted to Sophia, I was going to fuck her because I could. Because I was a Boss Bitch!

"Hey, Sophia. What did you think about the meeting?" I asked as we walked across the yard toward our housing unit.

"I always like the meetings. I learn so much. You and Sheena give good advice. Y'all are some of the smartest women I've ever met. And I like what you said about being a Boss Bitch. It's empowering."

"Good. We gotta help each other out. Be our sistah's keepers."

"Yeah. You're right. Um."

Sophia became quiet. I could tell she had something on her mind. "What's going on in that head of yours? Something on your mind?"

"Um. Yeah. Um."

"Spit it out, girl."

"I kinda have a crush on you." She blushed.

I couldn't contain my smile. "You wanna hear something crazy? I kinda have a crush on you, too."

"Really?" she beamed.

I decided to go for it all. It was now or never. "Yeah. Hey, you want to spend the night in my room tonight?"

She looked surprised by my question. "For real? I can do that?"

"Yeah. I'll get Jayda to stay in your room and you can stay in ours. We'll make the switch after dinner. The guards don't pay attention to who is in the rooms as long as two of us are in there. Third shift doesn't know who is who."

When I got back to my cell, I broke the news to Jayda. "I need the room for the night."

"What are you talking about?"

"I need the room for the night. I want to fuck Sophia."

"What? Who is Sophia?"

"A girl down the hall. Stop asking so many damn questions."

Jayda's eyes filled with tears. I could see the hurt and anger. "But why, Loretta? I thought we was good. I thought we had something going on?"

"Chill, Jayda. I told you, I don't want a girlfriend. We are friends, not girlfriends. Quit tripping."

"But what if we get caught? I don't wanna lose my job because you want to turn out some young bitch."

I didn't want to argue with her. Boss Bitches didn't argue. "You know third shift don't know who we are. Either you gon' do this or I'ma cell up with her. Your choice."

Jayda gave me an angry stare. I knew she didn't like me kicking her out for the night, but I wasn't giving her a choice. "Okay," she whined, giving in.

Sophia didn't take her eyes off me during dinner. She was sitting five tables away, and every time I turned my head in her direction, we made eye contact. She looked anxious and eager.

When I turned back to my left, I felt another set of eyes on me. Two tables away, Jayda was giving me a nasty look. She was jealous. I didn't like that. Jealous women blew up spots.

"Alright, ladies. Chow's over. Got five minutes to get back to your rooms," the C.O. called out.

After dumping our trays, Sophia and I walked to my cell while Jayda headed for Sophia's room.

"Welcome to the best cell on the block. Make yourself comfortable. I noticed you didn't eat that tuna salad. Want something to eat?" I offered, opening my locker. It was filled with all kinds of goodies. Chips, cakes, Ramen noodles, sausage logs, and cookies.

"Nah, I'm good. Had a big lunch. Not trying to get fat."

I sized her up as she sat on my bunk. I guessed her to be about 5'6" and 125 pounds. "You don't have to worry about gettin' fat. You got the kind of body all the models want. You weigh, what? 125 at best?"

"110," she corrected.

"Like I said, you don't have to worry about that. Plus, you're young. How old are you, anyway?"

"Eighteen."

"Damn. You're a kid. I was only twenty when I came in. How much time you got? Where you from?"

"I was born in Puerto-Rico, but we came to Wisconsin when I was five. To Madison."

"That where you caught your case?"

"Yeah. I stabbed my mom's boyfriend a couple times. He was touchy-feely. Got five years."

"That's what his ass gets. You should've cut his balls off," I laughed.

"I tried. Missed and stabbed him in the leg."

"Ouch! So, have you ever been with a woman before?" I asked as I sat on the bed next to her.

"Once, when I was in middle school. But we didn't know what we were doing."

"So, what made you choose me?"

"I like the way you carry yourself. And you're pretty with pretty eyes. Plus, I like your booty. Wish I had a booty like yours, but you see I have white girl genes. Little in the back, but big in the front," she laughed, palming her breasts.

I reached up and rubbed my hand across her breasts. "I think you're pretty. And you have nice titties."

"Thanks," she blushed.

"Just so you know, I'm not looking for a girlfriend. We can fuck around sometimes, but I don't want to be in love. I will scratch your back if you scratch mines. Cool?"

"Yeah."

And then it was on! I worked my tongue all over her body until she couldn't move and made her cum so many times she got dehydrated.

Chapter 4

"Hey, Sheena. You've been pretty quiet today. What's going on?"

"Today is just one of those days, Loretta. I feel like blah. I go through this every year around this time."

We walked in silence for a few moments. I wanted to know what the significance of this day was, but I didn't want to ask. So I waited. And while I waited for her to speak up, I looked around the rec yard. The yard was at least an acre, maybe two. Women were scattered all over doing all kinds of activities – playing cards, basketball, softball, tennis. Others were working out and running or walking past us on the track.

"My mother died today."

I heard what she said, but I looked over at her to make sure I heard her right. "Today? This morning?"

"Not today, literally. I meant this date. July seventh. Brain aneurism. She was my rock. Did everything for me, and then some. I miss her."

Hearing the pain and longing in Sheena's voice made me think of my own parents. I missed them, too. "I lost both of my parents, too. Five years ago. A car accident."

Sheena looked surprised. "Damn, Loretta. I didn't realize we had so much in common. Do you have any other family out there? All I have is my brother. He tries to be there for me, but he's in the army, so he's always gone. Hard to reach at times. But he does what he can when he can. What about you?"

I was hesitant to answer. I didn't want to get too deep, but Sheena had bared her soul to me, so I figured I owed her some reciprocity. "No. I don't have anyone. I mean, I have family, but I don't know them. I think my mom and dad moved to Wisconsin to get away, so I didn't get to know any of my family members on their sides. We visited them every now and then, like around family reunion time, but that was it. I have a baby out there, too. A daughter."

"What? Are you serious? Why haven't you told me any of this? Where are the pictures?"

"I don't have any. She was only a couple of months old when I got locked up. Right now she's in foster care. She was in the car when my parents died. The car seat saved her. None of my family members would take her, so they put her in the system. I don't know where she is, but I'm going to find her when I get out."

"Damn, Loretta. You've been through some shit, girl. Let's switch topics before I get to cryin' out here. How's the Boss Bitch thing coming?"

"I'm feeling it, Sheena. For real. It's been in my thoughts non-stop. The ideal of getting to that level is starting to set in. I'm even thinking about changing my name."

Sheena looked at me to see if I was serious. I gave her my poker face. "Oh, man! You serious, huh?"

"Yeah. I don't want to be the pretty, shy girl no more. I'm ready to grow. Evolve. I even started playing with a little pussy."

Sheena gave me a double-take. "What? You got some pussy? Seriously?"

Seeing her reaction made me laugh. "Yeah. Jayda and the young Latina girl, Sophia."

Sheena's eyes looked like they were about to pop out of her head. "You got two girlfriends? What? This Boss Bitch stuff is really going to your head, huh?"

"They're not my girlfriends. I made that clear. I don't want a woman. I'm not looking for love. I don't want the drama. I just want to get my rocks off and move on."

"Damn, Loretta. I can't believe I'm hearing this from you. You are turning into a Boss Bitch."

***

"But I am so horny, Loretta. Please! Can't we just get in a quickie?" Sophia asked, grabbing ahold of my hand as we walked up the stairs.

30

We were walking back to our rooms from recreation. My plan to turn her out had worked better than I thought it would. She was addicted, wanting to be my cellmate and girlfriend. If I didn't know any better, I would've sworn she was falling in love.

"Wait 'til tonight, girl. Chill. You trippin'."

"But my celly is gone right now. This is a good time. You can leave when they open the doors for showers."

I wanted to be mad, but I couldn't. Watching her was like watching a crackhead beg for a rock.

"No, Sophia. You can wait. Stop acting like that," I laughed

"Please, Loretta! I need it now. Please!"

I looked over at her and could've sworn I seen tears in her eyes. "Okay. C'mon."

She became giddy as a schoolgirl as we walked toward her cell. As soon as the door closed behind us, Sophia was all over me. I had to force her to lay on the bed so I could get her clothes off. I didn't even get a chance to take off mine before she pulled me on top of her.

I started at her big, pink nipples, fingering her as I sucked them. She went wild. I was kissing my way down her body, about to suck her pearl, when there was a bang on the door. I looked up and seen C.O. Anderson staring at us through the cell door's window.

Shit!

"Open cell twenty-three," I heard him say into his radio.

Sophia scrambled to wrap herself in a sheet as the door opened. I tried not to panic, but I couldn't help it. I knew I would be going to the hole for sure. Not only was I in the wrong cell, but he caught us having sex.

"Well, well, well! What do we have here?" Officer Anderson asked, smiling like he had won the lotto as he stood in the door. He was tall, white, fat, and ugly. I knew the only way he got pussy was to pay for it, which was exactly why he worked in a women's prison.

"What's up, Anderson?" I asked, trying to see how he would handle us. He didn't call it in on the radio, so I figured we had a shot at talking ourselves out of trouble.

"You were doing a damn good job, Miss Jones. I hate to have to send you guys to the hole, but I have to do my job. Unless you guys could somehow persuade me to keep my mouth closed," he grinned.

I missed dick, but I did not want to have sex with him. Not only had I never had sex with a white man, but he was fat and nasty. But I did have Sophia. I was about to see just how bad she wanted to be my girl.

"What did you have in mind, Anderson?"

He looked over at Sophia, who was doing a bad job of hiding under the sheet. "Hernandez."

I turned to Sophia and gave her a look that let her know she had to do it. "Sophia?"

She nodded at me. We had dodged a bullet. *Whew!*

"I'll go stand watch," I said, easing by him and out of the room.

"If anybody comes, you have to cause a distraction so I can get out of here," he said, a nervous look flashing in his eyes.

"I got it." I pulled the door up, leaving it slightly ajar.

For the next two minutes I tried not to be suspicious as I looked back and forth between the room and down the hall. The room eventually got most of my attention. When Anderson pulled down his pants, his pale, white, flat ass almost blinded me. When I seen what he was packing in the front, I couldn't help but laugh. He had one of the smallest dicks I had ever seen. Fully erect, he was only about four inches. And it was pink.

Sophia wasted no time getting with the program. She dropped the sheet, bent over, and knelt on the bed. He entered her from behind. After a few pumps, he pulled out and told Sophia to suck him. I could tell by the way his head leaned back that he came in her mouth. I almost threw up in my mouth. That shit looked nasty as hell.

Sophia was a trooper, and as if she was reading my thoughts, she spat his cum out on the bed. Anderson buckled his pants and walked out of the room wearing one of the biggest smiles I had ever seen.

"Thanks for watching. I'm going to see what you can do next. I've never fucked a black girl before. Heard you guys are freaks," he said, brushing his belly against me and grabbing my ass as he walked by.

"Yeah. Next time," I smiled.

"That shit was nasty!" Sophia spat as I walked in the room.

I didn't give a damn about the nasty taste in Sophia's mouth. I had already concocted a plan. I went right for the sheet on Sophia's bed. "Brush your teeth, girl. And tell Tasha to get you some new sheets."

***

Two days had passed since me and Sophia's encounter with C.O. Anderson. Every chance he got, he reminded me that I owed him. He had even set it up to be in my room at 12:30.

That was in exactly five minutes. I was sitting on my bed waiting for him in my panties and bra, all smiles.

"Hey, Jones," he grinned as he walked into my cell.

I spread my legs wide and ran my fingers across my pantied crotch. "Hey, big boy."

"Take those off. I don't have much time," he said, grabbing at his belt.

I didn't move.

"C'mon, Jones. Take 'em off," he said, stroking his little pink dick as he walked toward me.

I smiled up at him with a smile that rivaled the Joker's. "Change of plans, Anderson. Jack off for me."

He looked at me like I had just spoken another language. "What? Don't play fucking games with me, Jones. Let's go," he demanded.

I returned the look he gave me. "I'm not playing around. Beat your meat."

He turned beet red as he pulled up his pants. "You know what? Fuck you, Jones. Pack your shit. I'm calling a white shirt. You and your girlfriend are going to the hole."

"I wouldn't do that if I was you."

"Why? My word against yours. Who do you think they'll believe? Your ass is grass."

"I have DNA. You left it in Hernandez's room. She doesn't swallow."

His face turned ash white. "What? Yeah, right. Where is it?"

"I have it. Trust me. I wouldn't play with you. Now, do as I say. Masturbate."

Anderson looked stunned. He didn't know what to do, and I loved it. I wanted to humiliate him. I wanted him to know I wasn't the average inmate. I wanted him to know I was a Boss Bitch!

"I can't believe this shit," he sulked as his pants hit the floor. He was no longer hard, and while he pulled on himself, trying to get wood, I began talking.

"I thought long and hard about this, Anderson, and this is what I want you to do. Bring me in an ounce of weed. When that is gone, you will get me another, and so on and so forth. For trying to fuck me, you will be my mule."

His eyes bulged. "What? No way! You're fucking crazy."

"Well, I'm telling them you raped me. I have your DNA. Don't play with me. I want my weed tomorrow, or else."

"C'mon, Jones. Don't do this. I could lose my job or go to jail. Please."

He looked pathetic. Terrified. But I didn't care. "Pull up your pants and get out. I want my weed."

"You're deadly as sin," he grumbled as he pulled up his pants and left my room.

Seeing his fear excited me. I had dominated a man. I could not believe it. I felt so powerful. And not only had I dominated a man, I had dominated a correctional officer. I'd seen how they humiliated and degraded us, acted better than us. Some of them even raped us. But I had reduced Anderson to a shell of a man. I'd seen the fear in his eyes, and that shit turned me on.

I rubbed between my legs and felt my panties were soaked. I was horny as hell. When Jayda came back, I was going to make her suck my pussy all night long.

J-Blunt

Chapter 5

"Hey, Loretta. Can I holla at you for a minute?" Reen asked. Reen was a pretty brown-skinned girl whose cell was a couple doors down from me. We were both standing in line, waiting to get our passes signed so we could leave the unit.

"What's up, Reen?"

"Wait 'til we get outside. I don't want everybody in my business. Where you headed?"

"To the library to meet up with my girls," I answered, in the back of my mind wondering what Reen wanted to talk to me about. I had kicked it with her at rec a few time, but we never spoke about anything serious.

"You be messin' wit' Sheena an' 'em, huh? The Real Girls Crew, or something like that?"

"It's unofficially the Real Sistahs, but we don't want a name tied to our meetings. You know how the prison administration can get when they start hearing we're cliquing up and naming ourselves."

"I heard that. These white folks be trippin'," she laughed.

After getting our passes signed, we left the unit. When we were sure no one was in earshot, Reen spoke. "I heard you got weed on deck. What up?"

I looked over at her, trying to get a read on her face. I was looking for a tell. I didn't know her that well, so I was suspicious. I had only been selling weed for two weeks, and I never told her about it. I had only told a handful of people.

"What are you talking about?"

"C'mon, Loretta. I'm good. You know Jayda be kickin' it wit' my girl, Celeste. I can have my brother put a hundred on yo' books. You got me?"

I gave her a long stare. I never sold drugs before, so I wanted to keep my circle of clientele small to minimize my chance of being told on. "Okay. I got you. I'll give you a sack at rec tonight, and the other one when I get the receipt. Cool?"

"Yep. A'ight, girl. I'ma holla at you later."

After parting ways with Reen, I began going over my talking points in my mind as I headed to the library. I had been reading books by Iyanla Vanzant, and I wanted to introduce some of her literature and concepts to the girls.

When I got to the meeting, I spotted all of the girls at our regular table. "Hey, ladies," I smiled as I walked over. I got lukewarm greetings from most of the women. The only one who looked happy to see me was Sophia.

"Alright. Now that we're all here, we can chop it up," Sheena began. "Today's meeting was supposed to be about new concepts and authors, but something has come to the group's attention that we feel we need to address."

All eyes shifted to me. I got a funny feeling in my stomach and my armpits began to sweat. "Why y'all lookin' at me like that?"

They continued staring until Sheena spoke up. "Word on the grounds is you are hustling. That true?"

I looked at Sheena and then around the table. Everyone looked serious except Sophia. She looked just as confused as I did. "Where did you hear this?" I asked, not wanting to confirm or deny anything.

"Malissa is the one who brought it to me. So, is it true?"

I gave Malissa a dirty look before responding. "Yeah. I'm doing a little something, but it's not a big deal. A sistah gotta get her paper."

"It is a big deal, Loretta. None of us at this table are saints, but most of us agree that dealing is a bad thing. It destroys communities and families. It brings heat. If the guards catch you, they'll probably think we're all involved."

"C'mon, Sheena. It's weed, not crack. And I'm careful. I been doing it for two weeks and y'all just now finding out. I must be doing something right if the people closest to me had no idea."

"The point is not when we found out, but the fact we did. People are talking. It's only a matter of time before everyone knows what you're doing, and then the heat will come. We don't want to be caught up in that."

I got defensive. "I'm a Boss Bitch. I take my own weight."
"That's not the point, Loretta. We don't want the heat on us.
Plus, you knew you were doing something wrong, which is the
reason you hid this from us for two weeks. We are trying to be
righteous sistahs, Loretta. You know that. And we have a right to
not want to be associated with a drug dealer."

Ouch! That hurt. "So, what are y'all saying?" I asked, looking
around the table.

Malissa spoke up. "We want you to stop dealing."

"Or?"

Sheena took over again. "There is no love lost, Loretta. We
are sistahs. We love you, but we don't love what you are doing. It
will cause you and us problems. What if someone gets jealous or
tries to play you? What if they tell on you? If the guards find
enough weed, that could be a new charge. We don't want you to
go down that road, so we are asking that you stop. Either that, or
stop coming to the meetings. It's your choice."

I searched the faces of everyone at the table. The group was
important to me. In the last couple of months, these women had
become my family. My sisters. I loved them all, but none of them
were supporting me. I had already flipped an ounce and made
fifteen hundred dollars. Working a prison job, it would take years
to make that kind of money, but I had done it in a week. And now
they wanted me to give it up. "I hear y'all concerns, and even
though I don't like it, I understand what y'all are saying. The
concerns are legit, and y'all have a right to choose. And so do I.
The fact of the matter is, I don't have a support system out there.
All I have is me. The choices I make must be in my own best
interest. I can't walk away from my money. I love all of y'all, but
I have to be able to support myself."

No one spoke as I got up from the table. No words were needed. They had to stick to their principles and do them, and I had to
stick to my guns and do me.

I was almost out of the library when somebody called me.
"Loretta!"

I turned around and seen Sophia heading in my direction. I waited for her by the door. "What are you doing? You're not staying with the group?"

"The group won't be the same without you in it. You're the Boss Bitch, and I got your back 'til the end."

When I got back to my cell, Jayda was sitting up watching TV. "Hey, girl. You back early. Did they put us on lockdown again?

"Nah. I left the group," I sighed, plopping down on my bed.

Jayda bent down to look at me. "Seriously? You left the Real Sistahs?"

"Yep."

"But I thought you was one of the leaders. What happened?"

"They wanted me to choose between them and selling weed."

"Really?"

"Yep."

"Damn. That's messed up. Glad I never came to none of y'all meetings. Bitches think they better than everybody. Hos too righteous for me."

I cut my eyes at Jayda. I wanted to defend the girls and give Jayda a lesson in principles, righteousness, and standing up for what you believe in. But I didn't. I knew she wouldn't understand.

"Forget them. Tell me about Celeste and Reen. They good?"

"Oh, yeah. I meant to tell you about them. I forgot. Reen wanted two grams. She good. I knew she used to do business with Trina before she left."

"Alright. She hollered at me on the way to the library. Next time don't be forgetting to tell me about business. I don't want people approaching me and I'm blind to the reason. If you know, I should know."

"Okay, Queen of Sheba," she said sarcastically.

"I'm not playing around, Jayda. Don't forget no more."

"Okay, Loretta. Sorry. Dang."

"Hey, did Vega ever get that money to you?"

"Um. No. Not yet."

"I knew she was going to be on that bullshit. That's why you shouldn't have given it to her."

"She paid the first time. I thought she would be good for some credit."

"Not that bitch. She's a bully. From now on, let her come to me and get it. Cash on delivery."

"Okay. Sorry."

"Stop apologizing. That shit is weak," I said, disgusted by her. Jayda was my homegirl, but she wasn't a fighter. I knew the real reason she didn't get the money from Vega was because she was scared of her. Vega had been owing me for two weeks, and had I not brought it up, Jayda would've probably let me forget about it. But I wasn't forgetting.

I made up my mind I would get the money from Vega. I would approach her at rec. Tonight.

***

After serving Reen, I began looking for Vega. Her and two butches, who were just as ugly as she was, were in the weight room working out. I was hoping we would be able to handle this like grown women, but knowing Vega, it would probably get just as ugly as she was. And I was prepared for that.

"Hey, Vega. Can I holla at you for a second?" I asked as I approached her from behind. She was working the shoulder press. I couldn't help but notice she was lifting 180 pounds. I weighed 160.

"'Sup, shawty?" one of the butches said, looking me up and down as she spun to face me. Her name was Lynn, but everybody called her L.

"C'mon, L. You know it ain't that kind of party," I said, cutting my eyes at her.

She gave me an, 'oh, you caught me,' smirk. "Why you be trippin', Loretta?"

I ignored her and watched Vega pump out her last rep. "'Sup, Loretta?" she asked, dropping the weight stack as she stood. She

41

towered over me. Compared to her, I looked like a midget. Her muscles were engorged with blood and her sweaty t-shirt stuck to her muscles like a compression shirt.

"Can I get a word with you real quick?" I asked, trying not to look intimidated.

"Fo' sho. Walk this way."

I followed Vega as she led me toward a water fountain on the other side of the gym. "I wanna know if you got that C-note for that weed Jayda gave you a couple weeks ago?"

She gave me an irritated look. "For real? That's what you want? I thought you was trynna join the team."

"Nah. I'm good on that, but I do need my money."

"Yeah, yeah. Don't trip. I gotchu," she said, blowing me off.

I refused to leave. "When you gon' give it to me?"

Vega got mad. "Damn, Loretta! Quit fuckin' sweatin' me! I'ma pay yo' ass when I feel like it."

Her burst of anger scared me a little, but the thought of being played scared me even more. I knew if I let her get away with it, somebody else would try to play me next. That's how it worked in prison. Inmates exploited other inmates' weaknesses.

"Vega, I'm not trying to fight you, but I need my money."

"Move, bitch!" Vega said, shoving me aside.

I stumbled backward, almost falling. When I caught my balance, I looked across the gymnasium to see who had seen her push me. About fifty sets of eyes were staring in our direction. I knew I would have to put up or shut up. And if I shut up, I would be preyed upon.

"Hey, Vega?" I called as I dug into the waist of my sweatpants. She turned around just as I was pulling my weapon. It was a belt looped through a padlock. I knew I would only have one swing, and I would have to make it count. Or else.

Before she realized what I was grabbing at, I had the weapon out and cocked back like a whip. I swung as hard as I could. The lock connected with the side of her head, making her stumble backward. She was dazed, but she didn't fall.

42

She grabbed the side of her head to check for blood. Yep. She was bleeding a river. Her eyes bucked as she looked down at her hand and then back up at me. The initial look in her eyes was shock. That quickly gave way to rage.

"Parsons! Jones! Break it up!" the C.O.s yelled.

Vega ignored them and charged at me. I cocked the lock back to try and deliver another blow. I was too slow. Vega plowed into me and wrapped me up in her arms. She lifted me off my feet like a rag doll and slammed me onto the wooden floor. The wind rushed out of my lungs. I couldn't breathe. And since this was my first time in a fight, I had no idea how to defend myself.

I tried to throw a kick, but it was no use. She climbed on top of me, pinning me down, and then started punching me. I tried to cover my face, but she was strong and heavy-handed. Her fists broke through my guard easily. The blows rained down on me like lightning and thunder. I had never been hit so hard in my life.

It seemed like it took forever for the C.O.s to wrestle her off of me. And even when the punches stopped, it still felt like I was being hit. I knew my face was cut up. I could feel it.

"Jones, can you hear me? You okay?"

I couldn't make out the face because I couldn't open my eyes, but I knew the voice. It was Anderson.

"Yeah. I'm good," I mumbled.

"What the fuck is wrong with you? You have a death wish or something? You're crazy as sin."

J-Blunt

Chapter 6

Six Months Later

I ended up doing 120 days in the hole for my fight with Vega. And while I suffered the first and worst ass-kicking of my life, I wouldn't have changed a thing. Except hitting her again instead of standing there while she checked her damage. But I had learned a lot about myself from my fight, namely that I was stronger than I thought I was; and that women respected me even though I lost the fight. I had done what they dreamed about doing, but were too scared to do.

From that experience I had grown. Evolved. Transformed. I used the hole as a cocoon. I went in a caterpillar named Loretta and came out a boss-ass butterfly named Syncere – Syn for short. Got that from C.O. Anderson. And now, six months later, I was bossier than ever.

"Hell nah! Morris Chestnut is fine, but he ain't all that. I need me a nigga that look like The Rock," Jayda laughed.

Me, Jayda, and Sophia were walking the track at outside rec. This had become my circle since I had gotten out of the hole. I was still cool with Sheena and the rest of the girls. They were doing them and I was doing me, but there was no love lost, at least not on my end.

"Now, there you go. The Rock is a fine mu'fucka. I like Morris, but The Rock look like he will tear it up!" I giggled.

"My ideal guy is Ricky Martin," Sophia chimed in.

Jayda gave her the eye. "Psh. Girl, you trippin'. He too pretty for me. I don't want no man who spend more time in the mirror than me."

"I hear that. I'm not with that metro-sexual stuff. To me, that is gay. I need me a man's man," I added.

"Syn!" Someone screamed my name, interrupting us.

I turned and seen a woman named Andrea walking quickly in our direction. Andrea was light skinned, about 5'5" and 150 pounds. She was a cool chick who smoked a lot of weed. One of my best customers.

"What's up, Andrea?"

She waved me over. "C'mere. I need to talk to you for a second."

I left my girls and walked over. "'Sup, girl?"

"You gotta come see this shit. You ain't gon' believe what's goin' down," she said, shaking her head from side-to-side with a spaced-out look in her eyes.

I got a sinking feeling in my gut. I just knew it had something to do with some weed. "What is it?"

"C'mon. Just come with me."

"I'ma be right back, y'all," I told Jayda and Sophia before following Andrea.

She led me across the rec yard and toward the bathhouse's boiler room. I asked her several times what was going on, but she kept telling me to wait and see. The suspense was killing me.

When we got to the entrance of the boiler room, not only was I surprised to see the door was unlocked, but there were no C.O.s around. I knew the only way this door got opened was with a key. Something was up.

I followed Andrea into the boiler room and we crept to the back. I could hear voices. Women's voices. Some were taunting, some laughing, and someone was whimpering like an injured dog.

When we got the back of the bathhouse, I couldn't believe my eyes. Vega was on her knees, her arms spread east and west, tied to pipes. She was butt-naked, bloodied, and bruised. Rain and about eight of her girls were surrounding her. They had broomsticks, locks and belts, and soap wrapped in towels. Rain was getting her revenge.

"See how much of that broomstick will fit up her ass, Leslie," Rain ordered.

I stood with wide eyes and watched Leslie walk up to Vega and move the broomstick against her anus. Vega screamed, trying her best to get away from the broom. All she managed to do was wiggle. They had her arms tied tightly. She did manage to momentarily stop the broom from going up her ass.

"Stop moving, bitch!" Rain yelled, lashing Vega's back with the belt-lock weapon like it was a whip. Vega stopped struggling after five or six blows.

Leslie lined the broom up with her butt again and thrust it in. Vega screamed and jerked violently. Leslie continued pushing the broom deeper into her rectum.

"You gon' learn about fuckin' wit' Rain, bitch," Rain taunted, grabbing ahold of the broom and snatching it from Vega roughly.

Vega screamed again. Feces and blood covered almost half of the broom.

"Stick it in that bitch pussy and give her ass a yeast infection!" Monica, another one of Rain's girls, yelled.

I had seen enough. I didn't like Vega one bit, but I couldn't stand by and watch her be tortured. Rain and her girls were menaces, and they would probably kill Vega.

"Hey, hey, hey! C'mon, y'all! Chill!" I yelled as I emerged from the shadows.

Rain and her party looked surprised to see me. "What's up, Syn? What you doin' here?" Rain asked.

"C'mon, Rain. Let her go. She's fucked up," I said as I took in the entire sight of Vega. She looked up at me with tears in her eyes. She was literally scared to death. Her eyes were swollen, face bloody, lips swollen, and she had welts all over her body, not to mention her bleeding out of the ass.

"Fuck that, Syn. You know this bitch needs to be taught a lesson. She a big-ass bully. You should want me to fuck her up, especially after what she did to you."

"Y'all taught her a lesson, Rain. She fucked up. Look at her. Y'all gon' mess around and kill her."

"Bitch need to die," Rain spat.

"C'mon, Rain. Don't do this. Let me deal with her. Do this for me," I pleaded. If Rain killed Vega, we would be put on lockdown for months. That meant my money would be messed up and the entire prison would probably be searched for contraband. I had weed and money stashed all over. My losses would be huge. The last thing I needed was a lockdown.

"Can't believe you trynna save her, Syn," Rain said, looking at me in disgust.

"Not just her. Everybody. Just let me deal with her."

Rain stared at me for a few seconds. "Okay, Syn. She's yours. I'ma do this because I got mad respect for yo' ass. But a word to the wise, if your dog get off the leash, I'ma kill her ass. And then me and my bitches coming for the owner."

I decided to let Rain get away with the threat. The last thing I needed was a war with Rain and her crew.

When they turned and started leaving, I started untying Vega. "Thank you so much, Syn. Thank you. I'm sorry about—"

"Shh. Fuck that shit, Vega. We good." I didn't want to hear her apologies. Right now I was more concerned with her not dying.

"Thank you so much, Syn. I'll make it up to you. I swear," she cried.

"I put my ass on the line for you, Vega. You owe me."

Part 2: Hail Mary

J-Blunt

A Gangster's Syn 2

Chapter 7

It felt like déjà vu. Different courtroom, different judge, different year, but the same circumstances. It wasn't C-Money this time, but another man I was in love with was on trial fighting for his life. And I, for the second time in twenty years, had a front row seat to my lover's fight for freedom.

The courtroom viewing area was packed. Luke's co-workers, friends, and family were present, and so were the so-called 'victim's' friends and family. Then there was the media. The blood-sucking, story-telling, sensationalizing media. Luke's legal battle made national headlines. CPA TURNED KILLER! WORKER AT DAY, KILLER AT NIGHT! DR. JEKYLL AND MR. HYDE OF THE ACCOUNTING WORLD! I had heard and read it all, and now everyone was on hand to watch the seven-day trial's final act, closing arguments, and then deliberation.

All eyes in the courtroom were focused on the district attorney as he stood to take the floor. Mitchell Sellers was the best D.A. Milwaukee ever had. He stood about 5'10" and weighed about 240 pounds. His skin was pale, his hair salt-and-peppered, and his face was clean of any facial hair. But the attribute that worried me the most was his success rate. His prosecution record was almost flawless with a 98% conviction rate.

"People of the jury, today the people of Wisconsin are calling for you to do justice. The families of the victims, who have sat in these pews at every court proceeding, want justice for the deaths of their loved ones. And while Mr. Swanson didn't personally shoot them all, make no mistake about it, he is just as guilty," he said, flashing the jury a smile. "Contrary to the defense of his brilliant, high-priced attorney, this is not a case about self-defense. This is not a case about him and his friend coming to the aid of a damsel in distress. This case is not about a law-abiding citizen legally arming himself and terminating a life-endangering threat. This case is a type of vigilante street justice. This man, Luke Swanson, and his deceased friend, Reginald Banks, A.K.A. Trigga, armed themselves and killed three men in broad daylight.

The deceased, Trigga, killing two of the men before he died himself. We, the people, have shown Mr. Swanson's true character. Don't be fooled, jury. While he is a college-educated, five-figure salary-making accountant, he is also a ruthless thug. His brother, who is currently serving a life sentence in federal prison for being convicted under the RICO Act, was one of the biggest drug dealers this city has ever known. His deceased friend, Trigga, was a convicted felon who's name had come up in seven homicide investigations. And we have witnesses testifying of Mr. Swanson's brazen, broad daylight shootout with two men at his girlfriend's house in the city of Glendale. It is the people's opinion that Luke Swanson was involved in criminal activity, just like his brother. Why else would he be involved in three separate shooting incidents? They made attempts on his life at his job, at his girlfriend's house, and at his apartment. What kind of law-abiding citizen has these kinds of wild-west-type of gun battles? This is no Tom Cruise movie. He jumped in bed with real gangsters, and real people died. Luke Swanson is guilty of murder in the first degree, people. We must send a message to the murderous thugs of his kind that Wisconsin will not tolerate gangland slayings in our neighborhoods. The prosecution rests."

If I would have had a gun on me, I would have shot the D.A. dead in the middle of the courtroom. He had twisted up all of the facts. He had made Luke into Al Capone or Big Meech. I watched the faces of the white jurors as Mitchell Sellers spoke. I could tell they were ready to convict my Luke.

"What a sensational performance by the district attorney," Michael Thompson, Luke's dreadlocked, brown-skinned, tailored suit-wearing lawyer said as he stood to take the floor. "People of the jury, I am going to make this short and sweet. While the D.A.'s closing argument was entertaining and well-delivered, it was also mostly false and grossly distorted. I am going to apologize right now for not being able to entertain you in the way that Mr. Sellers did because, quite frankly, the truth is not that entertaining. But the truth is the truth. And the truth is Mr. Swanson shouldn't even be on trial. This case has nothing to do with the incident that happened in the plaza parking lot because my client wasn't even there. This also has nothing to do with his brother because Luke was away at college while Barron was on trial. What this case is about is a man who defended himself. A man who was shot twice in the chest and almost killed in front of his own home. A man who was almost murdered by a convicted felon in broad daylight. Three attempts were made on Mr. Swanson's life for reasons which Mr. Sellers didn't care to mention in his closing arguments. Mr. Swanson was targeted by this gang of hoodlums because he wouldn't commit a crime. That's right! Because he wouldn't do wrong, they tried to kill him. They wanted him to launder their money. Luke refused. And because he refused, they came after him with their guns blazing. What was he supposed to do? The American way is to defend yourself and your rights. This is a God-given Constitutional right. No crimes were committed by Mr. Swanson, and if protecting your life is a crime, then God help us all. The defense rests."

***

"So, what do you think, Syn?" Trinity asked as we walked down the courthouse steps.

"I don't know. I think if he had a jury of his peers, he would beat the charges. But when the D.A. was talking, I watched some of the white jurors' faces. They believed him."

"You gotta keep the faith, Boss Lady. Now is no time to have doubt. I have come to ever day of this trial with you, and I believe my man, Luke, is gonna walk. He killed the nigga who shot him. He's good," Bryce said as he escorted me and Trinity to the rented sedan.

"Yeah. You're right, Bryce. They need to hurry up and reach a verdict. I can't wait 'til he gets out," I said as visions of me running into Luke's arms like they did in the movies played in my mind.

"So, what did he say? Is he coming to California to live with us, or does he want to stay in Milwaukee?" Trinity asked.

We moved to the sunshine state right after Luke got arrested. Calico had my strip club and modeling agency burned down, and Luke ordered me to leave the state until he was finished with the legal system. I hated leaving my hometown, but me staying stressed Luke out. He had enough to worry about, so I moved to Los Angeles to give him some peace of mind.

"He doesn't have a choice. If I have to leave, so does he," I told her as we ducked into the car. "Besides, our club and studios out there give us a bigger market. It's better for business if we stay out west."

"Where to, Boss Lady?" Bryce asked as he climbed into the driver's seat. He was my chauffer and bodyguard while I was in town.

"Surprise me, big man. The lawyers have my number, so we'll know when the jury is ready."

"I think we should go do some shopping, Syn. Take some stress out of the wait. I know shopping always puts me in a good mood," Trinity spoke.

"Or working out. A good workout is not only healthy, but you can take out a lot of frustration. What do you say, Boss Lady? Wanna hit up a gym?" Bryce asked, flexing a bicep as he stared at me through the rearview mirror.

I gave Bryce's suggestion some thought as I stared at the back of his big, bald head. And while I was lost in making my decision, I realized he even had muscles on the back of his head and neck. How was that even possible?

"Nah, Bryce. I haven't worked out in years. I think I'ma go with Trinity's suggestion and go shopping. Plus, can't you use a new muscle shirt?" I cracked.

"See, you got jokes, huh, Boss Lady?" Bryce laughed as he navigated through traffic.

After sharing a laugh, the car became silent and I got lost in my thoughts about Luke. I wanted him home so bad. He had been in jail for nine months. Nine long, hard, and lonely months. The D.A. had convinced the judge not to give him bail, so my baby had to sit.

"Need to stop and get some gas," Bryce called, interrupting my thoughts.

After he parked at the pump, I got out to go pay for the gas, Trinity at my side. I was almost to the gas station's door when I seen the tan Chevy Avalanche parked at a pump near the door. There was a passenger still in the truck. A woman. I figured her husband was still inside. I started to head back to my rental car when Trinity's voice stopped me.

"Isn't that Luke's mother?" she asked, pointing to the truck.

"Yep. That's her. I'ma head back to the car. Can you pay for the gas? I don't have the patience to endure a run-in with them."

"Yeah. I'ma–"

When Trinity stopped talking, I looked up to see what had caught her tongue. Luke's father had walked out of the gas station. He was headed right toward us, except he didn't see us because he was looking at the phone in his hand. He looked up just in time to stop himself from running into us.

"Excuse me, young–" he was saying, but stopped talking when he recognized my face.

This was the first time we had been this close. I had seen him and his wife at all of Luke's hearings, but their body language made it clear they didn't like me or want to talk to me, so I avoided them and they avoided me. Until now.

Looking into Mr. Swanson's eyes was like looking into Luke's.

"So, you're just going to let my son go down for you, huh? What kind of woman are you? I know all of this is your fault."

I was kind of stunned by Mr. Swanson's words. They cut me. Deep. "I didn't get him into anything. I know Luke already told you what happened. They tried to kill us."

"That's bullshit! Luke didn't have anyone trying to kill him until he met you. You got my boy into this mess, and if he gets life in prison, it's your fault. You ain't t–"

"Martin, get in the car. Don't talk to that woman." I turned my head and seen Luke's mother walking toward us. "We know you got our son into this. God don't like ugly, Syncere. You don't have to answer to us, but you will answer to Him. C'mon, Martin."

I stood speechless and watched his parents head to their truck. Hearing their words hurt. Not having their approval was tough, but hearing the hate in their voices hurt even more.

"C'mon, Syn. Forget them. Don't let them get you down. Luke needs you to be strong," Trinity said, laying a hand on my shoulder.

I knew I needed to do like Trinity said and forget them, but I couldn't. They had increased my stress level by infinity. I no longer wanted to shop. I knew that wouldn't do the trick this time. "Bryce! Where is the closest gym?"

Chapter 8

It took the jury three hours to reach a verdict. I didn't know if that was a good or bad thing, but in a few minutes I would find out.

As I sat in the holding tank behind the judge's chamber, bits and pieces of my life played through my mind like I was watching it on a TV screen. Mom and Pop cheering from the sideline at my pee-wee football game. The proud look on Barron's face when I won the Golden Glove title. The media attention I got during my sophomore year in college when I made the game-winning steal to upset the best team in our conference, guaranteeing us a berth in the NCAA tournament. How I cried when I first held Latia, my daughter. The many congratulations I got when I was hired at the accounting firm.

And now the remainder of my life and all of my accomplishments were in jeopardy, held in the hands of a bunch of people the court said were my peers. If my peers believed the D.A., I could spend the rest of my life in prison. Just like my brother.

"Swanson!" the bailiff called from the other side of the door

"I'm ready," I said, standing and smoothing the wrinkles from my blue, tailored K&G suit.

When the door opened, the bailiff, a black man in his mid-forties named Jackson, put me in cuffs and led me down a short, dimly-lit hall. The door at the end of the hall opened up to the courtroom. I could hear the cameras clicking and see the flashes as I walked through the door. Hundreds of pairs of eyes were on me. The only eyes that mattered were those of my daughter, my parents, and Syn. I had to look around the court to find them because they were on different sides, as they had been at all of my hearings.

"So, what do you think?" I asked my lawyer as I sat next to him.

Michael Thompson, A.K.A. Mike, was one of the best lawyers in the state. He was highly regarded by my brother. Now I was hoping my brother's faith in him would reward me with my freedom. I hated jail.

J-Blunt

"Just like I said when we spoke in the back, I think you're about to walk. The D.A. spewed a bunch of bullshit with no facts. Hell, he twisted the facts. But we live in a pro-gun era, and I think you will get self defense." Mike looked and sounded confident. That gave me a little comfort.

"All rise!" the bailiff called as the judge entered the courtroom from his side chamber. Everyone stood.

"You may be seated," the Honorable Judge Jefferson Grahm called out as he took a seat at his bench. Judge Grahm was a 62-year-old white man with whitened hair and sunken facial features. He looked more like a rat than a human being. Mr. Rat Face had been on the bench for twenty-plus years. According to Mike, he was the fairest judge in the felony division.

"We are gathered here for the reading of the verdict. Are all parties present?" Judge Grahm asked, looking back and forth from my table to the district attorney's.

"All parties present, your honor," Bailiff Jackson spoke.

"Bring in the jury," the judge ordered.

The bailiff walked to a door on the far side of the courtroom. He ducked his head inside and said a few words. The twelve-person jury made up of five white men, five white women, one Hispanic woman, and one black woman marched into the room like robots. I searched their faces for a sign of their verdict. They all wore poker faces, and not one of them looked in my direction. The little comfort I had taken in Mike's words vanished.

"Jury foreman, have you reached a verdict?" the judge asked.

A bald headed white man stood to his feet. He was casually dressed in a polo shirt and slacks. "Yes, we have, your honor."

"What did you find?"

My heart started beating like a drum during a Native American rain dance ceremony, and I started sweating from places I didn't even know I could sweat.

"On the charge of first degree intentional homicide, we find the defendant guilty."

Gasps, swears, and applause reverberated in the courtroom, but I didn't hear anything. It felt like someone had stabbed me in the heart. I had been found guilty of the worst homicide charge possible. The sentence carried mandatory life. I couldn't believe it. I was never getting out of prison.

Mike grabbed ahold of my shoulder and whispered something in my ear. I couldn't understand the words. My body was numb, my senses distorted. It took a few minutes for me to shake the fog. And when by aural senses finally started working again, I heard the judge pass sentence.

Life with the possibility of parole in forty years.

***

I walked back to the unit in a trance. I didn't even remember changing from the suit and back into the orange jumpsuit. I didn't remember the elevator rides or the walks down the long corridors, didn't remember walking into the unit or into my cell, didn't remember putting on my headphones and turning on my AM/FM Walkman as I lay on my bunk. And when I fell asleep, I didn't even remember my dream.

I was woken by the loud music of a radio commercial blaring in my ears. A car dealer was saying something about the great deals he was giving for a limited time. When I opened my eyes, the first thing I seen was the white concrete of the underside of the bottom bunk. When I realized I was still in jail, my verdict reading began playing in my mind. I couldn't believe I got life.

I snatched the headphones off and powered off the radio as I saw up in bed. I felt disoriented. Like I wasn't myself. Like something inside of me was broken, but I couldn't put my finger on what it was.

Bits and pieces of the judge's sentencing spiel began playing in my mind. He called me a menace to society. A fraud. A thug.

Then sentenced me to life.

"Luke? You woke?" my cellmate called from the top bunk.

My cellmate's name was J-Murder. We had been roomed up for a couple of months. He was a member of the infamous Trigga Klan, a clique of shooters founded by my slain friend, Trigga. J-

Murder was only twenty, and like me, he was facing the rest of his life in prison for murder.

"Yeah. What up, Murder?" I mumbled.

"You good, fam?"

I could hear the concern in his voice. J-Murder knew my situation as well as most people. The streets had been talking, saying I used to be a square that got sucked into murder by a woman.

"Nah, Murder. They found me guilty. I got life."

"Damn, my nigga. That shit is fucked up. I thought you was gon' beat that shit. But you can't give up, my dude. It's plenty niggas that popped back on appeal. Fight that shit."

"I am. It's just fucked up hearing that verdict. I got life."

"Yeah, I hear you, my nigga. My trial start next month. I know if that shit don't go my way, I'ma be fucked up, too."

The room became silent.

"Manny and Cy got to talkin' big shit when you came back. Them bitch-ass niggas was happy you didn't go home. They ride that nigga Calico dick like they some jump-offs. Me and Yae was gon' smash them niggas, but I wanted to make sure you was good before I fucked around and went to the hole."

"Fuck them niggas, Murder. I got they bitch ass. Just worry 'bout 'yo shit. Worry 'bout beatin' that charge."

"Trust me, my dude, I'm on my shit. But I can't stand to see hatin'-ass niggas celebrate the downfall of a real nigga."

"Don't trip. They gon' get it."

We became silent again. I looked around the room until my eyes landed on a picture of Syn. It was in a frame made out of Doritos bags and sitting on the small concrete table next to the bed. Before all of the drama stared, I had only known her for a little over four months. And in a span of about 120-days I had fallen in love and traded my life for a cell.

"Yo, Luke? Can I ask you something?"

"Yeah. What up?"

"I got plenty of respect for you, and I don't want you to think I'm disrespectin' you, but I gotta ask..." He paused. I waited. "Why you didn't just stop fuckin' wit' Syncere? The streets say

Calico gave you a pass. That he just wanted her. Why you get in that?"

I thought long and hard about my response before I spoke. "Man, I been asking myself that shit for nine months, J. Everyday I wake up in here, I ask myself that shit. Big Chief got me the pass even after I murked one of Calico's niggas. But shit, Syn was my girl. I was already so deep in the shit that I wanted all or nothin'. Me and Trigga had a plan to murk Calico. Syn didn't even know about it. But he got to us first. I know that probably sound like some sucka shit, but I couldn't let Calico off my girl."

"I feel you, Luke. On some real shit, I wouldn't let a nigga touch my bitch, either. That shit just fucked up. I know yo' moms an' 'em fucked up about that shit. They lost two sons to the joint."

I hadn't even thought about my mom and dad until J-Murder brought them up. I knew that verdict messed them up as much as it did me. I was the son who was supposed to have beaten the streets. The son who validated their good parenting. The son they could be proud of.

But now all of that had changed. I had become their worst nightmare. I had become just like my brother.

J-Blunt

Chapter 9

"Swanson, visit!"

I opened my eyes, regretfully remembering I was still in jail. My body cracked and popped as I sat up in bed. Last night was rough. I couldn't get any rest, and when I dozed off, I was awakened by the foreman reciting that damn verdict. Life. Parole eligibility in forty years.

Shit!

I lumbered out of bed and grabbed my toiletry bag. After freshening up at the sink inside the cell, I went out to the dayroom to see who had come to visit.

The first thing I noticed after I closed my door was Manny and Cy. They were playing dominoes at one of the dayroom tables. Manny was a light-skinned dude in his late twenties with gold teeth and stood about six feet. His counterpart, Cy, also in his late twenties, was short and dark-skinned with a bald head.

When they seen me, they stopped playing dominoes and put on their practiced hard faces. I mugged them back as I walked across the dayroom and up to the visiting booths. When I got to the booths, I looked at the thirteen-inch monitor and seen my parents' terrified faces. The stress from my trial had aged them both. Mom looked like she had been crying for weeks, and my father looked sad and confused.

"Hey, Pop," I spoke into the small speaker mounted at the base of the screen in front of me.

"Morning, son. How are you?"

"I don't know, Dad. I thought I was coming home, and now I'm not. I knew the case was serious when they denied me bail, but I guess I expected my self-defense argument to prevail. Didn't think I would be going to prison."

"Just hang in there, son. I talked to your lawyer yesterday, and he's already starting the appeal process. He says you have some appealable issues. Did you talk to him yet?"

"Nah. I haven't talked to nobody. I didn't even use the phones yesterday. All I wanted to do was sleep."

"Yeah. When you didn't call, we got worried. That's why we're so early."

"I'm okay, Pop. I'ma roll with the punches and see what happens."

"Just hang in there, son. We have your back. Your mother wants to speak."

"Luke. Oh my God, baby! I was so worried about you. Why didn't you call last night? How are you doing."

"I'm doing better than I expected. And the reason I didn't call was because I went to sleep. Didn't feel like talking. I'm probably depressed or something."

"You stay strong, baby. We are praying for you. The whole church. I know you're not what that demon district attorney said you were. You're a good boy. God will see you through this. I know He will."

"Yeah. Tell everybody I said thanks for the prayers. And I got the Bible, too."

"Good. Now, how much do you think it will cost for the lawyer to work on your appeal?"

"Don't worry about that, Mom. Me and Syncere will figure that out."

At the mention of Syncere's name, my mom's angelic face turned into an angry mask. "You need to get away from her, Luke. Me and your father will help you out. She can keep her sin money. I know she is the reason you are in here. I can feel it. She owns a strip club and her nickname is Sin. Before she came around, you were fine. Me and your father figured it out. They came to her house looking for her. And they came to her modeling place looking for her. I don't know why you're taking the blame for all of this, but you need to stop and tell the truth. Me, your father, and your daughter are suffering because of your silence."

I didn't know how to respond to what my mom said. A part of me felt she was right. If I would have told the police about the $100,000 Syn owed Calico and told her to give the police the security footage from the club, it probably would've helped my defense. We could have told them about the drug king who tried to bully and extort her, and maybe had some witnesses back it up. But I knew that would've led to more questions, like what happened after the security footage showed me beating up the Hawaiian and running toward Syn's office with the gun. And why the Hawaiian's friend was never shown leaving the club. All it would have took was one of Syn's workers or club patrons giving a statement, then it was possible I would've been fighting another murder charge. So I took all the blame, not only to protect Syn, but to protect myself from another murder charge.

"C'mon, Mom. I told you she didn't have anything to do with this. She is good. Trust me."

"I don't care what you say, Luke. I will never like her. I know she got you into this. You can lie to everyone else, but you can't lie to me."

After the visit with my parents, I decided to use the phone. I needed to give Syn a call. I knew she was probably just as worried as my parents were, and now that I already had my visit for the day, I needed to make the call all the more since I probably wouldn't be seeing her for a while. The prison van could come and get me any day, and I didn't have a clue how visiting worked in prison.

As I walked down the stairs, I was met by the ugly stares of Manny and Cy. I hated them. I knew they were cowards – flunkies, really – and I knew if they kept pushing me, I was gonna whip one or both of their asses. But in the meantime, I got my mean mug on as I headed to the phone banks, which happened to be just two tables away from where they were sitting.

"Bitch-ass nigga gon' get his soon as he get up north," Manny smirked.

"Fag-ass nigga betta be focused on not droppin' the soap," Cy cracked, laughing like they were watching stand-up comedy. I tried my best to ignore them as I listened to Syn's phone ring.

"Him and his bitch-ass brother got life. Two less ho-ass niggas the streets gotta worry 'bout."

"Luke! Baby, I'ma video visit you right now. Why didn't you call me last night? I sat up–"

"Listen, Syn. Don't visit. My parents already did. I'm okay. Don't worry about me. I can't talk that long right now because I'm 'bout to whoop these bitch-ass niggas. I'ma call you when I can. I love you."

"Luke! Wait! I don't–"

I hung up before she could finish. When I spun around, Manny and Cy were mugging me. They were about ten feet away. Still at the table playing dominoes. I decided to beat Manny's ass first. He said the shit about me and my brother, and he was the biggest. I covered the distance between us in three steps. I moved so fast Manny didn't have time to stand. He was a sitting target by the time I got to him. When my fist connected with his chin, he tipped over in his chair. I didn't have time to check the damage because Cy had jumped up.

"Stop fighting!" I heard the sheriff's deputy yell.

Too late for that. Cy was already taking a swing at me. I couldn't stop now, and after easily dodging his wild punch, I tore into his ass. "Talk that shit now, bitch-ass nigga!" I said as I gave him a one-two. "Laugh now, pussy," I said before connecting another combo.

Cy didn't talk or laugh. I seen fear in his eyes. He knew he couldn't throw down with me. His final move to try and get me off his ass was throwing a wild haymaker. I dodged it easily. "You fight like a bitch," I mocked.

"Stop fighting!" the deputy yelled again.

I ignored the deputy and threw a fake jab at Cy. He flinched, dropping his guard to block the imaginary blow. While his guard was down, I landed a right hook to his jaw. His knees gave out. Down goes Frasier!

I was turning to find Manny, getting ready to finish him off, when I seen a blur out of the corner of my eye. Manny's fist was flying at me. I didn't have enough time to move. The punch landed on my temple. It dazed me. I stumbled backward and dropped my guard. He charged at me.

Before Manny could get to me, I seen another blur, this one moving toward Manny. J-Murder dove on him like he was sacking a quarterback.

I was about to go help J-Murder stomp a hole in Manny's ass when something seized me. I heard a loud crackle as my body stiffened. I fell to the ground and began shaking uncontrollably as the volts from the Taser surged through me.

J-Blunt

Chapter 10

One Year Later

I couldn't wait to see my man. Even though I talked to him on the phone every day and had been seeing him several times for the last year, I never lost the excitement I felt every time I seen him. I was in love with Luke. Full-blown I-would-die-without-you-in-my-life love. And just because he was locked away in prison and the judge had given him life, that didn't mean I was going to stop loving him. He had given his life to protect me. He had shown me the highest form of love possible by sacrificing his freedom for me. For that, I owed him. And I would spend the rest of my life making down payments of love and devotion to him and catering to all of his needs.

Luke was locked up in Waupun Correctional Institution, a maximum-security prison in Waupun, Wisconsin. According to the judge, this is where he would die. As I waited for my baby to come out to visit, I let my eyes roam across the visiting room. The room was big, about the size of a YMCA gymnasium, and most of the space was filled with plastic chairs and tables so small they only came up to my knees. I was praying Mike could work a miracle and get Luke out on appeal, because I didn't want to spend the rest of my life seeing Luke in this room.

When I heard the click of a lock, I looked toward the door where the prisoners were let into the visiting area. The door swung open and Luke came out. Every time I seen him, it felt like the first time. My heart fluttered and a smile as big as the sun spread across my face. I stood to receive him as he strolled coolly toward me. Even in a green prison khaki suit, my man looked good. His hair was always freshly cut, he was always clean-shaven, and his skin had a beautiful, healthy glow. The muscles he had been putting on were the icing on the cake. His prison greens were baggy, but every time I hugged him, it felt like I was hugging some type of African God.

"Hey, baby," he smiled, licking his lips as he wrapped me up.

"Hey, love," I cooed, getting lost in his strong arms. We always hugged before we kissed. I had this thing about resting my head against his chest. I always wanted to touch him before I kissed him, but after I got my fix from his touch, my lips found his. Our kisses were a combination between 'I miss you' and 'I want to fuck you.' Soft and rough. Sloppy and wet. But always perfect.

"You smell good," he smiled as he sat in his assigned seat. Inmates had to sit facing the guards' station.

"It's Salvatore Ferragamo. I thought you might like it. So, how are you doing today?"

"I was doin' a'ight 'til I seen them damn pants you got on," he said, giving me a once-over.

My visiting attire was always something form-fitting. Today I wore a camo shirt, a tight-fitting pair of jeans, and Chelsea Paris pumps. I had to make sure to give him a good show. Not that he was missing much. I always sent him tastefully seductive pictures in thongs and bras. I would've sent him naked pictures, but the prison wouldn't allow it.

"Guess what? I don't got on panties, either," I said, opening my legs so he could see my front wedgie.

"Ooh, shit! When this is all over with, I'm fuckin' you for a week straight."

"I'ma hold you to that, too. I need you to keep it up for a week."

"Trust me, baby. That won't be hard. So, how is everything with the apartment? You and Cynthia good?"

"This apartment is temporary. It's cool because its only three blocks from you, but I'ma buy a house soon."

"What about the house in Cali?"

"We keeping that, too. Trinity is keeping it up and running the businesses while I'm here. She is invaluable. Almost like having two of me. When I come to spend the week with you, she steps perfectly into her role as me."

"So, when do you think you gon' tell her you're really her mother?"

"I don't know, baby. To be honest, I like things the way they are. She tells me everything and trusts me like I'm her friend. If I tell her I'm her mother, I'm scared things might change."

"Yeah, they probably will change. But Trinity is cool. I actually think she will be able to handle it. She is strong. Like you."

"Yeah. I know. I'll tell her one day. Just not ready yet. Enough about my daughter, how is your daughter?"

"Latia is good. Coming up with her mom once you leave town. Gettin' big. And she smart as ever."

"That's good. I'ma have to talk Shay into letting me keep her one of these summers."

"Good luck. Shay hate yo' ass," he laughed.

"She just jealous because you love me. You didn't put that bitch on your visiting list, did you?" I asked, giving him the evil eye. He told me she had been asking to see him, and I was against it.

"Nah. I ain't trynna kick it with her like that. Too much drama. If it wasn't for my daughter, I wouldn't even talk to her ass."

"Good, 'cause I don't want her ass trynna fuck in mines. I don't care if you fuck all the female staff in this prison, just don't start back talkin' to her trifflin' ass."

"You good, Syn. Crazy-ass," he laughed. "Speakin' of crazy, what's up with Cynthia crazy ass? She still trippin'?"

"Lord, don't get me started. I know you like her, but I'ma have to leave her ass."

"What? Why?"

"She getting too attached. I told her I wasn't lookin' for love or a relationship at the beginning. She knows I love you, but the other day she brought up us gettin' a civil union."

Luke looked surprised. "For real? She trynna get married?"

"Yeah. Like I wanna marry another woman. I'm changing my last name once: when you get out. She got me thinking about crossing back over to men."

"Nope," he said flatly.

"I know. I'm just playing. But I'm about to find another girl. But forget about me. How are you?"

"I'm good. Calico flunkies still pretending like they want a war, but you know me and my niggas stay ready."

Two years ago, hearing Luke talk about warring would have been foreign, but now that he was in prison, he seemed to be getting harder. Everyday he stayed in prison was moving him further from an accountant and closer to a thug. I still wasn't sure if that was a good or bad thing.

"Be careful, baby. Make sure you keep somebody with you. Wolves prey on the sheep that ride solo," I advised, recalling the lessons I learned while in prison.

"Look at you, giving me advice on how to survive in prison," he smiled.

"I did seventeen years. I know how it is."

"Yeah, I know. But this shit is gon' end one day. One day that nigga Calico gon' get his. Then we gon' see how his groupies act."

I didn't respond to Luke's comment. I didn't have to. Luke knew I wanted Calico dead just as bad as he did. Neither of us would be safe until he had a funeral, and I wanted to be the one to put him in his grave.

"You haven't been back down to Milwaukee, have you?" he asked, interrupting my thoughts on Calico's funeral.

"No."

"Good. That nigga still lookin' for you. Stay out of the city. It ain't safe. The Trigga Klan gon' give him his issue soon. I can feel it."

***

After my three-hour visit with Luke, I left the visiting room and headed over to the lobby to get my purse and cell phone from the visitor lockers. I had just turned in my key when I saw a face that made me do a double-take. She was standing in the middle of a group of about seven or eight correctional officers.

"Ferrary!" I called.

The woman looked up from the sea of blue shirts and in my direction. It was her.

"Syncere? What are you doing here, girl?" she asked as she walked over to give me a hug.

"I just came from visiting. What are you doing here?" I asked, looking her up and down. She looked alien wearing the light blue C.O. uniform.

"I'm training here. Just started last week. And my name is Tahiti. After the club burned down and you left town, I had to find something to do. Ended up going back to school for criminal justice. Now, here I am."

"Wow. Who would've imagined," I chuckled. "But I am impressed. I couldn't take all of y'all with me. Sorry. But I see you managed to land on your feet."

"I did. So, who are you seeing?"

"Luke," I said, recalling our goodbye kiss. I hated leaving him behind.

"Luke is here?" she asked, the surprise evident in her eyes.

"Yep. Been here for about a year."

"Wow. Small world. Well, I have to clock in. Give me your number and maybe we can get together."

After exchanging numbers with Tahiti, I left the prison and hopped in my blue Kia Sorrento and headed home. My temporary home was an apartment three blocks away. I hated living in Waupun. It was small, white-populated town where everyone knew everyone. I was the only black person for miles. The only time I seen other black people was in the visiting room when I visited Luke. So, whenever I was in town, I normally stayed in the apartment and caught up on work, talked to Luke, and watched TV. Occasionally I brought Cynthia along to help with my boredom. One thing was for sure: when I bought my house in Wisconsin, I was buying one in Beaver Dam. The town was about twenty minutes from Waupun, but I didn't mind. I knew there were a few more black people in Beaver Dam, so I wouldn't feel so alien.

"Hey, Syncere," Cynthia said dryly as I let myself in the house. She was sitting on the couch wearing a tank top and booty shorts, her face glued to her tablet.

"Hey. What you up to?" I asked as I sat next to her.

Cynthia was fine. Movie star fine. Light skin, big brown eyes, long curly hair, and a body the white men of California went crazy for. Big, fake 36DD breasts packed onto a 5'3" and 120-pound frame. She was a workout freak and lived in the gym. I met her during one of my modeling agency casting calls in L.A. We hit it off right away, and when I told Luke about her, he gave me the green light. He was against me dating men, but I could eat all the pussy I wanted.

"Nothing. Facebook. How was your visit with *Luke*?"

I could hear the disdain in her voice when she said his name. I immediately got an attitude. "What the fuck is your problem?"

"Why are you still flying halfway across the country to see a man who is never getting out of prison? We could be spending our time doing other stuff. This is boring."

"I told you that you could have stayed your ass in L.A. You don't have to be here. And for your information, I will keep flying halfway across the country to see *my man* until he comes home. If you don't like it, you can leave. You're not my woman." I had to be this way with Cynthia, had to hit her hard with my words or else she would get beside herself.

"I'm sorry, Syn. I didn't mean it like that," she apologized, setting down her tablet and reaching out to me.

I slapped her hand away. I was angry. "Don't give me that bullshit. You always pulling this shit. I told you from the jump that we would just be friends. I'm not in love with you. I don't want a wife. There is no relationship. If you can't handle that, you need to find someone else."

"Don't talk to me like that, Syncere. I said I was sorry. I just don't understand why you're wasting your time on someone who is never getting out when you have me right here."

I wanted to slap her ass. "You know what, Cynthia? Get the fuck out! I'm not about to keep going through this shit with you. Better yet, I'm leaving. When I come back, you better not be here. And when I get to L.A., your shit better be out of my house."

After leaving the apartment, I hopped in my SUV and headed for the highway. I had too may things on my plate to be constantly arguing with a possessive, insecure woman. I could do bad all by my damn self. Arguing with Cynthia made me think about Luke's stance on me not getting a man. I was tired of clingy women. Plus, I could really go for a hard dick. I hadn't had the real thing since Luke left almost two years ago. I missed the strong touch of a man, but I couldn't lie to Luke or betray him. He had shown me the truest form of love and loyalty by sacrificing himself for me. I realized my loyalty to him was much more important than a piece of meat. So, until he was free, I would do without.

As I rolled the highway, I thought about what Luke said about Calico. He needed to die, sooner rather than later. I was tired of running, and I was tired of Luke having to fight his cronies in prison. I wanted Calico's ass dead yesterday. Luke had a lot of hope in the Trigga Klan killing him, but they were taking too long, so I started developing my own plans. I hadn't told Luke anything. I knew he would try to stop me if he found out. So I took a note from his book and kept my plan of killing Calico to myself.

I would succeed. I wasn't going to let Calico get to me first. I was going to *Don Killuminati: The 7 Day Theory* all of my enemies. And I was saving Calico for last.

J-Blunt

A Gangster's Syn 2

Chapter 11

"See, Luke, we have constitutional rights, and any time those constitutional rights are violated, you can petition the court and say, 'Hey, y'all violated my rights.' They gotta take what they call an independent look at that shit, meaning they have to do their own investigation of the facts. You feel me?" Big Ham said as we walked across the prison yard. Big Ham's name fit him to a tee. He was 6'4" and 300-something pounds, and he looked just like a really black version of The Hamburglar from the McDonald's commercials they used to show in the nineties. Big Ham was also a certified paralegal. If he could've taken the bar exam, I'm sure he would've been better than Johnny Cochran.

"Yeah, I hear you, man," I nodded, keeping my eyes on the two dudes who were walking about 25 feet ahead of us. Their names were Money and Buck. Money stood about 6'3", weighed about 200 pounds, was dark-skinned, and wore his hair in brushed waves. Buck was about 5'6", chubby, and as black as tar with his hair in French braids to the back. Both of them were Calico's groupies.

"Now, see, in your case, yo' due process rights were violated because... Ay, you even listening to me, man?" Big Ham asked when he noticed I was giving him only half of my attention.

"Yeah, I hear you," I responded, looking back and forth from Big Ham to Calico's groupies. They had slowed down to almost a snail's pace, like they wanted me to catch up to them.

"Who them niggas?"

"Some of Calico's flunkies. You see how they slowin' up?"

"Yeah. Is that Buck?"

"Yeah. That's his bitch-ass," I nodded.

"You got a shank? You know that nigga keep a poker."

"Yeah. Just got this new wooden one today." In prison, shanks were like pistols. No matter how small or weak you were at fighting, if you had a shank and you stabbed someone in the right spot, they were going down. I had just gotten a new shank made of

77

wood. Now I didn't have to leave it behind when I went to places behind the metal detectors.

"Good, 'cause I don't. My shit metal, so I had to leave it in the stash. If it go down, you take Buck. I got the tall nigga."

"Yep," I mumbled, keeping my eyes on my enemies.

When we were a couple of feet behind them, me and Big Ham slowed our pace, not allowing them to get behind us. I knew they were cowards, and cowards liked to strike when someone had their backs turned.

"'Sup, Luke?" Money asked, turning and mean-mugging me.

I kept my mug on and didn't speak, looking him up and down like he stank.

"I see niggas got they practice lookin' hard faces on," Buck cracked.

I wanted to punch him, and I would have except a C.O. had popped out of one of the gun towers and began watching us.

"Saved by the bell, nigga," Buck muttered before him and Money walked away.

"Them niggas got so much bitch in them that they don't need no females. They probably got pussies," Big Ham laughed.

"I'm tired of this shit, man. Calico got all these niggas around here on his dick. I'ma fuck around and have to kill one of these niggas."

"Luke, as yo' friend and legal advisor, I say you should let one of these niggas that don't got a chance at going home do that shit for you. You got a good issue. If you catch a body in prison, you gon' fuck up your chance. You still got a shot at this appeal. Don't fuck it up on some pussy-ass niggas."

"Yeah. I hear you. I'm just tired of these niggas trynna spook me. I want to show these niggas I ain't no accidental murderer."

"I hear you, Luke, but you have a good shot at getting back out. Pay them niggas back by gettin' out and fuckin' they mommas or somethin'. Put that shit on the internet."

Even though I was mad, I had to laugh at Ham's suggestion. It wasn't bad at all.

78

***

When I got back to the unit, me and Big Ham split up. The Walls, A.K.A Waupun, was divided into four main cell halls: the North, Northwest, South, and Southwest. They had an extra unit for crazy people, but I didn't know much about that. The cell hall I was housed in was the Southwest. Each cell hall held about 300 inmates on four tiers. The top two tiers were all single rooms. That's where I was headed until I heard someone call my name.

"Swanson!"

I stopped on the middle of the first stairwell and spun to see who had called my name. It was C.O. Johnson, one of the two black female guards that worked at the prison. I was sure I knew her from somewhere, but I wasn't sure where.

"'Sup, Johnson?"

"Come here. You have mail."

I walked over to the officer's desk and seen her going through a stack of mail.

"You have some big booty girl magazines, a letter, and two newspapers: a *Milwaukee Journal* and *USA Today*."

I wanted to stay and try to talk to her, get a feel for what she was about. Not only was she a fine and thick redbone, but she had a booty that made a nigga dream about her. Problem was, she had a fan club. C.O.s and inmates were constantly jocking to be in her presence. Since I didn't want to be a part of the fan club or be mistaken as a thirsty nigga, I got my look on and kept it moving.

"A'ight. Thanks, Johnson," I said, about to turn and leave.

"Hey. Wait."

I stopped to face her. "What up?"

"Let me get a pat search."

My heart sank deep into the pit of my stomach. I still had my shank on me. I couldn't let her search me. If she found my shiv, I would be going to the hole for at least three months. "C'mon, Johnson. I'm all sweaty an' shit."

"Boy, stop playin' and get over here. I ain't finna bite you," she said, putting on plastic blue gloves as she walked toward me.

For a moment I considered running. Problem was, I was in prison and didn't have nowhere to run. Plus, if I ran, C.O.s from all over the prison would come to chase me, and after they caught me they would question why I ran. And wherever I tried to throw the shank, they would find it. And that would only add to my charges. I figured my best bet was to let her search me and hope she missed the shank. If she did find it, I'd try to talk my way out of it by playing the 'we are brothers and sisters' card.

"C'mon, ma. Why you wanna search me?" I stalled, looking toward the sergeants' cage on the other side of the cell hall to see how many guards were around. Only Sergeant Bizmark was there, and he wasn't paying us any attention because he was on the phone.

"I need to search you because I heard you had a big weapon," she smiled.

I didn't know if she was flirting with me or if Money or Buck told on me, but because she smiled when she mentioned my big weapon, I was hoping she was flirting. So I spread my feet apart and stretched my arms east and west. She started from my ankles.

"Where are you coming from?" she asked as she felt up my right leg.

"Rec," I answered, trying not to sound nervous.

"And what were you doing at rec?" she asked, working her way up my left leg.

"Working out."

"I can tell." And then, out of nowhere, she reached around me and grabbed my dick. I thought I was tripping. "Hey!" I flinched, looking around to see if anyone seen what she did. No one was around except the Sergeant, and he was still on the phone.

"Hmph. My tip was right. You do have a big weapon. And big arms. Ooh, and a nice chest."

I spun around to face her. "Where I know you from?"

C.O. Johnson just stared at me. She looked good, like a mix between Nikki Minaj and Raven Simone. Her long hair was pulled into a ponytail, and she had a body like one of the girls in big booty magazines.

80

"You really don't remember me, Luke?" she asked, smiling at me like I was a contestant on a game show.

"Nah. You look familiar, but I'm not sure."

"I gave you a lap dance before."

She used to be a stripper. That was only a small help. I had gotten lots of lap dances, not to mention Syn owned a strip club.

"When? Where? Refresh my memory."

"I'm Ferrary. I used to work for your girl."

I thought some more, but still didn't remember her. Lots of girls worked for Syn, and they were all fine and thick.

"Trigga's party. Lap dance by the bar. I thanked you for her."

I remembered. "Oh shit! Ferrary!" I yelled way louder than I intended.

"Shh! Yes."

I couldn't believe my eyes. "So, this is yo' new profession, huh? A C.O.?"

"Yeah. For now. I seen Syn last week after she visited you. I been trying to work over here so I can see you. How are you doing?"

"Shit, I don't know. I haven't had my dick grabbed by a woman in damn near two years, so right now I'm feeling things I haven't felt before."

"Boy, stop!" she laughed. "I talked to Syn and she supposed to be coming back to town next week. She said she wanted me to do something for her, but she didn't say what. I heard she started the modeling agency and strip club out west. I'm hoping she wants to hire me back, because I would love to live out in Cali."

"Yeah. We're doing big things out west. Haters made it hard for us in the Mil. But damn, C.O. Johnson is Ferrary. I can't believe this shit."

"I had to do something after Syn left, so I went back to school. But can you keep my past between us? I don't want these thirsty-ass niggas around here all in my business."

"Don't trip, Ferrary. I would never do nothin' to jeopardize yo' livelihood. I don't fuck wit' mosta these niggas, anyway. I'm hopin' this shit is temporary. I got business to tend to out there.

J-Blunt

"All right. You gotta go now. I'ma be seeing you around. When you talk to Syn, tell her I said hi."

"Will do."

82

A Gangster's Syn 2

Chapter 12

I pulled the black Charger to the curb and cut the engine. It was almost one in the morning, and the residential block looked deserted. No lights were on in any of the houses on either side of the street. Perfect. I climbed out of the car and closed the door silently.

After one last look down the block, I adjusted the black baseball cap, making sure my hair was hidden, and pushed the big bifocals further up my nose. When I began my walk up the walkway, I put on my best B-Boy strut. I was hoping my dark, baggy jeans, 3x shirt, and walk would make anyone who happened to be looking think I was a man.

Once I was upon the porch, I rang the doorbell and waited. A few moments later I heard movement on the other side.

"Who is it?" a woman's voice called.

I didn't answer, just rang the bell again.

"Who is it?" the woman called again as she fumbled with the locks.

"I'm looking for Rhoda. She here?" I asked, making my voice as deep as I could.

The door swung open and a light inside the house clicked on. Rhoda stood in the doorway. She was blacker, fatter, uglier, and older, but it was her.

"Do I know you?" she asked, clutching at her robe as she peered at me from behind the screen door.

"It's me, Loretta. Can we talk?"

At the mention of my name, her eyes popped and jaw slacked. "Loretta? Is that you, for real?" she asked, opening the door to get a better look at me.

I stepped closer, letting the light from the inside reveal my facial features. "Yeah. It's me. Can I come in?"

"Yeah. Sure. Come in," she said, taking a step back and letting me in.

I made sure not to touch anything as I walked past her.

"Damn, Loretta. I can't believe it's you. Why did you come by so late? And why are you dressed like a man?" she asked as she closed and locked the door.

"This is me now," I said, looking around as I stepped into the house. The living room was decorated with purple furniture, hardwood floors, and a big TV on the wall. I knew she lived alone. I had stalked her for weeks. And as I stared at her, it wasn't hard to see why she lived alone. She was every bit of 300 pounds.

"Oh my God, Loretta! I can't believe it's you. When did you get out?" she asked, looking happy to see me.

"I been out for a couple years. Been trying to get myself re-established out here."

"Was that you I seen at the apartment complex a couple of years ago? Back then you were dressed like a woman."

"Nah. I ain't wit' that dress shit. I go for comfort now," I lied.

"I swear I seen somebody that looked just like you. So, what's up? Why didn't you come over a little earlier? How did you even find out where I lived?"

"Everything is on the computer nowadays. And I'm here because we need to talk."

"Okay. Sit down. What do you want to talk about."

I didn't accept her offer to sit. "Why did you get up on that stand and make me look like a monster? You knew I needed your help, Rhoda. Why did you do that to me? I thought you loved me? I thought we were friends?"

Her tears came quick. "I'm sorry, Loretta. I am. If I could take it back, I would. I was confused and missing Rasheed. His family was pressuring me. I was hurting, girl."

Parts of her testimony played in my mind as I stood before her. "But what about me? What about my daughter? Did you think about us? What about us being friends? Rasheed tried to rape me, Rhoda. Didn't that matter?"

"I didn't mean to do it, Loretta. They kept harassing me. I'm sorry for everything."

84

I was tired of her apologies. Hearing her whine and seeing her tears made me angry. I needed to wrap this up and get the information I needed.

"Where does Calico live?"

She looked surprised by my question. "Who? What? I-I don't know who that is," she stuttered.

Hearing her lie to me got me madder. "Where does Calico live, Rhoda? Stop bullshitting."

"I-I don't know what you're talking–" She stopped talking when I pulled the silenced .38 Special from my waist. "Loretta. Please. I don't–"

"Where does he live?" I asked, pointing the gun at her.

"I swear, I don't know. Please. Please, don't shoot me."

"Why didn't y'all just leave me alone? Why did you have to fuck with me? Why did you tell him I was out?"

"It wasn't me, Loretta. I don't even know who Calico is."

"He told me it was you, Rhoda, right before he sent his people to try to kill me. That was me at the apartment building. You knew it, and you told him I was out. He tried to kill me, Rhoda. You fucked me over twice."

"Loretta, please. I swear I didn't know he would try to hurt you. He kept talking about the money after Rasheed died. I was still mad at you for killing him. I loved him. So, when I thought I saw you, I found a way to get in touch with him. I didn't know he would try to kill you. I just–"

Clap!

The .38 bullet tore into her forehead, knocking her to the floor. I stood over her and watched the life slowly fade from her eyes as blood pooled behind her head. I didn't feel bad about killing her. She had already died to me the day she testified for the state against me. This morning was a literal manifestation of her death.

As I left her house, I felt satisfied that I had watched her die. I actually smiled at the thought of her knowing I had killed her. Payback was a bitch. A bitch named Syn.

***

"So, what do you like better, being a dancer or a C.O.?" I asked Tahiti as I took a sip of my Long Island Iced Tea. We were seated at the bar of a popular nightclub in Dodge County.

"I made more money as a dancer, but the benefits from being employed by the state are great. Medical, dental, 401(k). But shit, when I'm walking around and got 1,300 horny niggas lookin' at my ass, it kinda feel like I'm back in the club," Tahiti laughed.

Tahiti was a cutie-pie. As I sat next to her watching her laugh, I tried to figure out why I didn't take her to Cali with me. She had everything my clubs represented. Fine, thick, sexy, and sassy. And just knowing she had a backup plan when stripping didn't work out made me like her all the more.

"So, how is my baby doing?" I asked, wanting the inside scoop on Luke.

"He's good, from what I can tell. I know he carries a shank. I don't get to work his cell hall that much because they say I cause too many distractions, but I don't care. I'm only training there. I'ma get transferred to Racine as soon as my probationary period is over."

"What would it take for you to stay at Waupun?" I asked, spinning on my barstool to face her.

"What? Why? I need to be around black co-workers. I mean, I'm half white, but I know I fall under the one-drop rule. Those white people don't want me in Waupun."

"I want you to stay there and be there for Luke. Watch out for him. Some people in there want to hurt him, and I can't let nobody fuck with my man. You can be my eyes and ears… and *hands*," I said, putting emphasis on the part about being my hands. I knew hunger bred strange appetites, and the last thing I wanted was my man developing an appetite for ass. Plus, I wanted to get him some pussy to try to make his prison stay as comfortable as possible.

"What are you saying, Syn?"

"What do you think I'm saying?"

"It sounds like you want me to fuck Luke."

"Yes. Among other things."

A Gangster's Syn 2

"I don't know, Syn," she said hesitantly. "I could lose my job and go to prison. Do you know that they charge prison guards with rape if we get caught having sex with inmates? I'm not trying to go to prison."

"I know. I did seventeen years in prison. I know how it goes."

She looked shocked. "Really? You did seventeen years?"

"Yeah. I just got out a couple years ago. We'll talk more about that later. Right now, I just want you to know I need your help. Guards have sex with inmates all the time. I seen it with my own eyes, and I know if don't nobody say nothing, they won't know nothing. Luke is not going to say you raped him. And even if you get caught and lose your job, I'll give you a better job."

Tahiti was silent. I could tell she was mulling it over.

"I don't know, Syn. You my girl, but, this is some heavy shit. They spooked us at the academy about going to prison."

I had her on the ropes. She just needed a little more encouraging.

"I'll tell yo what. If you get caught, I will give you $50,000 and a job. And, if you agree right now, I will also throw in $1,000 a month."

Her eyes popped like I had just told her she won the lottery "Seriously? You'll give me $50,000?"

"Let me make this clear, Tahiti. I'm going to give you $1,000 a month to take care of Luke. If you get caught, I will give you fifty-thousand-dollars and a job."

"Shit, where the fuck do I sign at?" she cracked.

"You crazy, girl. No signatures. I'll take your word. And before the night is over, I'll give you a thousand dollars. That means you start tomorrow."

"Trust me, taking care of Luke is not a hard job. Your man is fine, and he got a nice body and a big dick."

I gave her the side eye. "How do you know about his dick size?"

"Remember, I gave him a lap dance to thank him for you at Trigga's party. I also kind of felt him up the other day during a pat search. That's how I knew he had a shank."

87

I gave her a lingering stare. "A'ight. Betta watch yo'self, girl. Luke is taken. Don't you fall in love with my man," I warned. I said it in a playful tone, but I was dead serious.

"I love money, Syn. Luke is your man and my job."

Her response brought a smile to my face. "Good answer. Bartender! Give us two shots of Patron!"

By the time we left the club, me and Tahiti were buzzing really good, and I, for one, was horny. Just thinking about Luke fucking her excited me. Me and Luke had never had a threesome, but I knew if Tahiti stayed around for the long haul, that would change as soon as he got out.

When I pulled into my apartment's parking lot, Tahiti pulled her gray Camry into the parking space next to my Kia. She had come back to my place to get her money, but I was going to try to get her to spend the night. I wanted to sample the goods before they got to Luke.

"Come in and make yourself comfortable. I'ma go grab the money," I said after I let us in the apartment.

I walked back to my room and grabbed the small safe out of the chest. After counting out ten $100 bills, I headed back into the living room. Tahiti was bent over, looking at pictures. She was wearing a pair of tight pink leather pants and heels. Her ass looked like a giant peach. I wanted to take a bite.

Then something happened. For the first time in my life, I got turned on by the sight of a woman.

"Here you go. See something you like?" I asked. walking up behind her and handing her the money.

"Nah. You gotta invest in some porn, girl. But thanks for the money. Kinda reminds me of my stripper days."

"I wished I could have taken all of y'all with me. I do. But I couldn't. I had to leave fast."

"I understand. But I landed on my feet. See?" she said, striking a sexy pose.

I couldn't take my eyes off of her. And if I didn't know any better, I would think she was flirting with me. "What do you have going on tonight?" I asked, letting my eyes roam over her body. She had crazy curves.

"Sleep."

"Do you have anybody waiting for you at home?"

"Nope. I don't do relationships. Just date. No kids. No curfews. I go where I want, when I want."

I didn't even try to hide my smile. "My kinda girl. Since you don't have anybody at home, why don't you stay with me tonight?"

Her eyes lowered to sexy slits. "And do what?"

I closed the distance between us, wrapped my arms around her, and palmed her ass. It was soft and jiggly. "I want some of what you're about to give my man."

I didn't wait for permission to kiss her. I just dove in. Tahiti kissed me back. Our lip-lock was aggressive and filled with lust. Our clothes came off quickly as we made our way to my couch. Neither one of us were wearing panties, so we wasted no time getting down and dirty. I climbed on top of her in the 69 position.

Her pussy was clean-shaven and wet, and it smelled like strawberries. I fingered her while I sucked her pearl. She did the same to me. My orgasm started bubbling fast. Tahiti was good and knew how to suck pussy. When I came, it was glorious. It felt so good that I stopped eating her and rode her face. She stuck her tongue inside me and I rode it until I came again.

After my second orgasm, I got off of her and gave her some solo attention. I loved the way she moaned as I ate her, and when she came, it was music to my ears.

"Wait right here," I told her as I got up and went to my room. I came back a few moments later with 'Luke'. Her eyes lit up when she seen the strap-on.

"Ooh, that looks so real."

"This is Luke. I had it made to look exactly like Luke's dick. So, this is what you'll be looking forward to."

She sat up and began fondling the fake penis as I strapped it on. "I like Luke."

I moved it to her mouth. "Show me."

Tahiti had no inhibitions. She sucked Luke like it was real, giving me eye contact the entire time. That shit was super erotic.

"Turn around," I said, pulling Luke from her jaws.

She spun around and knelt on the couch. I admired her ass as I got behind her. It was fat and round, one of the best asses I had ever gotten behind.

"Mm, shit!" she moaned when I slipped Luke in.

I kept going until most of it was in, then stopped to let her walls adjust. "How does it feel?"

"That shit feels good. Quit playin' around and fuck me, bitch."

I started with slow, deep strokes, exactly how Luke used to do me. I gradually picked up speed, and before long I was dickin' her ass down. I slammed my pelvis into her ass as hard as I could, her booty cheeks jiggling violently every time I thrust forward.

"Oh yeah, Syn! Fuck me, bitch! Fuck me!" she screamed, throwing her ass back at me.

I spread her cheeks apart so I could go deeper. "Call me Luke."

"Oh shit, Luke! Mm. Yeah, baby."

Hearing her call me my man's name got me so excited that it felt like I was about to cum. "Say it again. Say it again."

"Oh yeah, Luke. Fuck me, Luke!"

I dicked Tahiti down until her body went stiff, and when she came, it was loud. I knew my neighbors heard us, but I didn't care. I had just found my new playgirl.

Chapter 13

"You into boys yet, little lady?" I asked my daughter as she tried her best to keep her Uno cards held tightly against her chest. My mom had brought Latia to visit. I couldn't help but notice how fast she was growing. I seen her twice a week every other week, and it seemed like each week that passed without me seeing her, she grew taller and more mature. Puberty hadn't started yet, but I knew it was coming, and that scared me.

"She better not be," my mom cut in.

"Ma, that's not gon' help. You gotta let her express herself. That's why I didn't tell you I was into girls when I was her age."

Mom gave me the eye as a surprised look spread across her face. "You were into girls when you were nine?"

"Yeah. Dad knew."

"You told your father and not me?" she asked, feigning hurt.

"I couldn't tell you, Ma. You was gon' beat me with the Bible."

"Sure was. You shouldn't have been thinking about girls at that age. You were supposed to be focused on school."

"I was. The girls were at school," I cracked.

"I don't like boys, Daddy. They stupid," Latia cut in.

"That's good, baby. Keep it that way."

"Amen to that," Mom added.

"But just in case you do find a boy you like, would you tell me?" I asked, wanting to keep the lines of communication open between me and my daughter.

"Yeah. I wouldn't lie to you, Daddy. Granny said lying is a sin, and you said you hate liars. I don't want to sin, and I don't want you to hate me."

I couldn't do anything but laugh at my daughter's naiveté. Her innocence was still beautiful to me.

"Have you heard from Barron lately? How is he doing?" Mom asked.

"He's good. I wrote him about a week ago. I should probably be hearing from him sometime this week. Has he reached out to you and Dad?"

"Since you've been gone he calls the house more, but he talks to your father the most. He says he's tired of me mentioning Jesus. Had the nerve to call my savior a prophet the last time we talked. I would've liked to chase him with a belt when he said that."

"He's Muslim, Mom. That's what they believe. You can't change that, no matter how many times you bring up Jesus."

Mom gave me a stern look. "Why are you saying this, Luke? You thinking about becoming a Muslim, too?"

"Nah. I still read the Bible you sent me and go to church sometimes."

"Good. Stay away from Islam. Jesus saves. Muhammad don't."

When the visit with my mom and daughter was over, I was put in a cage and strip-searched. No matter how many times I got strip-searched, I still couldn't get used to the process. The shit was humiliating and dehumanizing. I hated lifting my nuts and spreading my ass cheeks for another man to inspect. I couldn't wait until I got my court decision back. Hopefully everything Big Ham told me would come true.

I left the visiting room and the high sun and warm temperature immediately reminded me what I was missing out on. I wanted a glimpse of the outside world badly, but the 40-foot castle-like walls that surrounded the prison blocked all hope of that. They called Waupun "The Walls" for a reason. All we could see from the inside of the prison was the sky.

I was looking at the clouds when I spotted C.O. Johnson heading in my direction. "What's up, Ferrary?" I grinned.

"Boy, don't be callin' me that while I'm here," she admonished, looking around to see if anyone was in earshot.

"Chill, girl. You good. You know I ain't gon' do nothin' to get you popped off. I love lookin' at yo' ass. I'ma miss it when you transfer."

"What if I told you I wasn't transferring?"

92

"I would say yo' ass is crazy. I know you wanna be closer to Milwaukee and around more black people. You and Sears the only black females that work here, and her ass so Oreo that she really don't qualify as black."

"Stop. Leave her alone. She cool," she laughed. "But I'm staying here. For real."

"What? Why?"

"I seen Syn last night, and-"

"What? Syn in Wisconsin?"

She looked like she got caught with her hand in the cookie jar. "Yeah. She's here. She's supposed to be coming to see you tomorrow. Don't say anything. I'm not supposed to be telling you any of this. It's supposed to be a surprise."

"Syn coming to see me is supposed to be a surprise?" I asked, wondering why I was supposed to be surprised.

"No. I'm the surprise. I'm staying so I can be here wit' you. To take care of you."

"Word?" I asked, unable to stop the smile from spreading across my face. I knew her taking care of me meant exactly what I thought it did.

"Yeah. C'mon. Let's walk to your unit so we don't draw any attention. I can't be just standing here talking to you. Too many people be in my video."

"So, when do you officially start taking care of me?" I asked, watching her ass sway and bounce as she led the way to the southwest cell hall.

"Well, I did just pick up some overtime. I'm working your cell hall on third shift."

"Don't be fuckin' wit' me, Ferrary."

"Call me Tahiti. That's my name. I'm not a stripper no more. And I'm not fucking around. I'm serious. Syn explained everything to me. You and her are my priorities. This is something like a relationship, I guess. Except Syn told me not to fall in love with you. So, I guess I'm like your girlfriend's girlfriend."

"Damn, I love Syn. My Boss Bitch is a beast!" I smiled, wishing I could slap Tahiti's bouncing ass.

"Now you have two Boss Bitches. Here's your stop. Don't get in any trouble. I'll be seeing you later tonight."

"A'ight." I watched Tahiti's ass bounce and jiggle as she walked away. When she looked back over her shoulder and seen me watching her, she put an extra switch in her hips. I didn't know how I was going to do it, but when I got the chance, I was fucking the shit out of Tahiti.

"Swanson, you have mail up at the desk," a white male C.O. named Strong called when I walked into the cell hall.

I stopped to pick up my mail. I had a couple newspapers and magazines and a letter from Barron. After walking up the four flights of stairs, I walked down to my cell: number 26, the last cell on the tier. My cell was small, about the size of a broom closet, fifteen feet long and seven feet wide. Only enough room for a bed, toilet, sink, and shelf.

After setting the magazines and papers on my bed, I opened Big Chief's letter.

Luke,

What's good, li'l bro? Every time I mail one of these damn letters to you in Waupun, I feel a little pain in my stomach. And it ain't gas, either, nigga. I hate that you in there. You was doing good 'til you started fucking with that she-devil. Yeah, Mom and Pop told me what they think about her, and you already know how I feel about her. I told you to leave her when y'all came to see me. This the kinda shit that happens when you allow people to stay in your life longer than they're supposed to. Some people are seasonal. I learned that from the mistakes I made. I kept seasonal people around past their due time and they turned state on me. Now you in the same boat. Guess we are brothers.

So, how is that appeal coming along? You said Big Ham and Mike found some solid issues. You got a word back from the courts yet? They shoot most niggas down on they first go-round, but don't give up or get discouraged.

Keep fighting. We Swansons. Giving up ain't in our blood. And keep yo' wits about you, too. I know Calico got flunkies all over. Just remember you got more to lose. And I liked what you wrote about fear. I agree that the presence of fear doesn't indicate the absence of faith. But hear me on this, li'l bro: faith can overcome fear. It's been my experience that they wrestle together. Sometimes fear can fuel you to overcome something impossible. Feel me?

All right, man. I'ma get this to you. Keep yo' eyes open and remember: we have eyes to see the truth in their eyes; we have ears to hear what they don't say.

Chief

After reading Big Chief's letter, I grabbed my pen and pad and sat at the table.

Chief,

What's up, bro? I just came back from seeing Mom and Latia. This little girl is getting too damn big. I have to get back out there. I'd hate for her to have to grow up without me.

Yeah, Big Ham and Mike say I have good issues. Still haven't heard from the courts yet. They say I should hear something soon. My hopes aren't too high, but I still expect to get love or some type of justice. But no matter what happens, I won't give up. I can't.

Being in this place is revealing strengths and insights into my character that are priceless. The other night I was sitting back listening to slow jams when it dawned on me that I've changed. I'm not who I was two years ago. I don't know what I've become, but I know I'm not the same. I've changed without knowing how or when, and I don't even have the words to describe it. Everything I used to want, I don't want anymore. I don't need love, I need loyalty. I don't need admiration, I need respect. I don't need fame, I need success. I don't need followers, I need believers. And I don't need help, I need an opportunity.

I like what you said about people being seasonal. True shit. Only problem is that don't apply to me and Syn. What you, Mom, and Pop don't understand is the intimacy that satisfies the soul is far deeper than the cravings of lust that satisfy the flesh.

Bro, I love and respect you to the nth degree. I know you've always had my best interests in the front of your mind, but what you all have to realize is I'm old enough to make my own decisions. Life is ten percent what happens to you and ninety percent how you respond to it. I'm not in here because of Syn. I am here for protecting what is important to me. I am here because I won't let nobody harm those I love. I learned that from you. Your exact words were, "If you don't do anything for love or to show love, then you don't love at all." The Bible teaches that sacrifice is the truest form of love. So, what do you advise? Should I not give everything I am to protect what I love? Or should I just stop loving her?

A'ight, bro. Take care of yourself and get at me when you have time. And the next time you call home, talk to Mom. She's asking about you.

Tried by fire, but never burned,
Luke

After I finished my letter to Barron, I decided to skip dinner and catch up on sleep. I didn't know how my night with Tahiti was going to go, but I planned on being woke all night long to see.

***

"Luke! Wake up."

When I opened my eyes and seen Tahiti standing in front of my cell bars, I got happy. "Hey, girl. I was just dreamin' about you," I said as I sat up in bed and stretched.

"Hope it was a good dream."

"Best dream I ever had," I laughed.

"You crazy," she giggled. "Come here. I have something to tell you."

I got out of bed and walked over to the bars. She pressed her body against them and began whispering in my ear. "I'm making my rounds every thirty minutes. When your neighbors fall asleep, it's on. Gimme a kiss."

There was a five- or six-inch gap between each of the bars, just enough room for me to get some of my face between them. As we kissed, I reached through the bars and palmed her ass. The kiss and her ass felt almost as good as Syn's. Almost.

When she broke the kiss, I felt like a newborn being disconnected from its mother when the umbilical cord was cut.

"I gotta go. Be back in thirty minutes." She walked away quickly. My eyes followed her bouncing ass until she was out of eyesight.

My dick was so hard I probably could've stabbed somebody with it if I used it as a weapon. It took everything inside me not to jack off when she left. Somehow I managed to keep my hands to myself until she returned thirty minutes later.

"Your bitch-ass neighbor still woke," she whispered.

"Send is ass to the hole," I joked.

"I should. I'ma be back later, but before I go, get naked."

I did and stood in the middle of my room like I was posing for a magazine spread. I even flexed a few muscles.

"Ooh. I like. What happened to your chest?"

I looked down at the two circular scars on the right side of my chest. "War stories."

"Let me get a picture for Syn," she said as she pulled out her phone. I didn't object. I even struck a few more poses. Then she was gone.

When she came back thirty minutes later, I was still naked.

"Damn. His punk-ass still woke. Look, my pussy is so wet. Feel it."

I reached my hand through the bars and went down the front of her pants. When I felt her wet pussy, precum dripped from the tip of my dick. I pulled my fingers out and sucked her juices off. It tasted like syrup.

"Let me taste," she said, giving me a seductive stare.

I stuck my index and middle fingers into her mouth and she started sucking. She even reached into my cell and gave my dick a few strokes. This woman was a freak!

"That's a preview. Be back."

She was back thirty minutes later, and this time my neighbor was asleep.

"He sleep, Luke. C'mere," she said in an excited whisper.

I ran to those bars like my cell door was being opened and I was going home. She pulled my dick through the bars and got on her knees. When her lips wrapped around my pole, a shiver ran through my body and a guttural moan forced its way out of my mouth. I took about twenty seconds to bust my first nut. Shit felt so good that I got light-headed and my knees almost gave out, but Tahiti didn't stop sucking. She swallowed every drop. My dick stayed hard and Tahiti kept sucking.

My second nut took a little longer, but not much, and again, Tahiti drained me. And my dick was still hard.

"Damn, Luke. How many nuts you got in there?" she asked as she got to her feet.

"Wait. Where you goin'?" I asked, wanting more.

"I gotta finish my round. I'ma be back in thirty minutes. My pussy is so wet, Luke. I want to fuck you so bad," she whispered before walking away.

I was irritated by the thirty minute rounds, but I understood she couldn't be gone from her post too long, so I sat on my bed, dick hard and throbbing, and waited. Thirty minutes later, she was back. I ran to those bars like a dope fiend running to the crack house on payday.

"I wanna get fucked, Luke, but don't go crazy, nigga. I can't make no noise. Okay?"

"Yeah, yeah. C'mon," I rushed her. I didn't want a pep talk. I wanted to fuck.

She gave one last peek into my neighbor's cell before turning around a pulling down her pants. I wasted no time pulling her ass into the bars. When she bent over, I shoved my dick into her as far as I could go. There were no words to describe how good her pussy felt. All I knew was I never wanted to pull out.

After I got past feeling the greatest feeling I had felt in two years, I clamped my hands on her hips like they were vise grips and went to work. I ignored her request to take it easy and let my hunger take over. I stroked her hard and fast. It didn't take long for me to bust a nut, but I didn't stop. I ignored the pain from my pelvis slamming into the bars as well as her nails digging into my wrists. I was in the zone!

"Luke, stop," she whispered.

I couldn't stop. She tried to break away from my grip, but I wouldn't let go. She stood up straight, but that still didn't stop my flow.

"Luke. You. Are. Going. To. Get. Me. In. Trouble." she whispered in between breaths.

I ignored her. My fourth nut was coming on strong, and I couldn't stop now. Tahiti hung in there like a champ until I exploded. I didn't know if anything came out, but it felt like the life had been drained out of me.

"What the fuck is wrong with you, nigga?" Tahiti whispered angrily, jerking away from the bars and pulling up her pants.

"My bad, Tahiti," I mumbled, wiping the sweat from my brow.

She gave me the meanest look she could muster. I know it was supposed to intimidate me, but it didn't. It got me excited. She looked sexy mad.

"'My bad' my ass. You gotta stop when I say stop, nigga. I could lose my job."

"Okay. That was my bad, for real. Come here, and let's kiss and make up," I said, reaching my hands through the bars.

She slapped my hands away and started down the tier. "Fuck you, Luke."

***

"So, how did you like my surprise?" Syn asked after we hugged and kissed. She had shown up to surprise me like Tahiti said.

"Is this visit the surprise, or Tahiti?" I asked as we sat.

"Both. Really Tahiti. So, what do you think?"

Visions of last night flashed in my mind. "Best present I ever got."

"Do you like her?"

I thought about how to answer the question. I really liked Tahiti, but I didn't want to tell Syn that. Me having sex with another woman was a new aspect of our relationship, and I didn't want her to get jealous. "Yeah. She's cool."

"Good. Because I like her, too."

I raised a brow. "Really?"

"Yeah. She's fine, sexy, and down to ride. And she don't seem like the clingy type."

"That's good. I think she might be mad at me, though. Did she tell you?"

"Yeah. And I can't blame you. It's been almost two years since you had some pussy. She lucky you didn't break her ass in half and pull her through those bars," she laughed.

"Tell her I said 'my bad.'"

"Don't worry, baby. She's good. I already kissed it and made it better."

Images of Syn eating Tahiti's pussy flashed in my mind and got me excited. "Damn, I love yo' ass, girl."

"Awe, I love you too, baby. And the picture. Mm, damn, baby. I'm thinking about making copies and framing them mu'fuckas on the walls at home, the club, and the modeling agency."

"Hey, if you want all your peers and employees breaking down these walls to free me, then be my guest," I laughed.

"Yeah. You have a point. On second thought, I think I'll just keep that in my phone. Speaking of phones, Tahiti is going to bring you one today. That way I won't have to keep paying those high-ass phone bills. Plus, I can send you videos and we can FaceTime.

"Yeah. Good idea. And I can check those stocks. The USA Todays are good, but it will be better if I can have more access to move stocks. But the good news is our money is growing."

"Yeah, yeah. Good. More stocks, more money. Right. But I don't care about that right now. Finish telling me about last night. And don't leave nothing out."

J-Blunt

Chapter 14

"Syn, I say we take the two on the left and the one in the middle," Trinity said.

I looked over the women as I gave Trinity's suggestion some thought. There were ten women standing before us in a mixture of ages, races, and sizes. The three girls Trinity had pointed out were gorgeous. One was white and looked to be about 5'8" and maybe 130 pounds. She had an athletic build with red, curly hair. The woman next to her looked Asian, 5'3", and 110 pounds. The girl in the middle was a light-skinned black girl who was built up like Serena Williams. Everything on her was big and muscular.

"Okay," I agreed, taking a few notes on my pad. Trinity had gotten good at scouting new faces. Our tastes were similar, and not only that, but she was proving to be an invaluable asset to me. She could fill in for me at any of my jobs at any time, and my businesses wouldn't miss a beat. She was good. She reminded me of me.

"Okay, ladies. Wait in the other room and we'll get in touch with you shortly. Marsha, can you send in the next group?" I told one of my assistants.

After the group of women left, another group of ten women came into the room. They were also a mix of different ages, races, and sizes. I was doing a casting call for my modeling agency, Synful Desires. I had about fifty girls under contract, and I was looking to add more. Most of the girls I worked with were considered plus size urban models, but I lacked the runway model types. I had just gotten a contract with a fitness brand, and they wanted athletic and runway model-type girls to represent their brand, so I rented out the event room at the Hilton and had a casting call. About 150 girls showed up.

Trinity and I managed to pick thirteen. After we had our girls, I went into the conference room to announce our decisions.

"Okay, ladies. Can I get everyone's attention? I want to thank you all for coming out to meet with us. I think all of you are beautiful, but unfortunately we don't have enough room for everyone. These are the names of the ladies we've chosen: Adrianne Miller, Bethany Hendricks, Alejandra Martinez, Tocarra James, Christy Schumer, Dana Reid, Samantha Grassley, Anne Sessions, Tamika Sergeant, Cam Nelson, and Jennifer Talbert. Thanks again to all of you who came out. I'm sorry that today wasn't your day, but keep trying and don't give up. I wish you all the best of luck."

After the girls we didn't choose left, Trinity handed out contracts to the thirteen chosen and I explained what the contracts stated. When they all agreed, I promised I would be in touch with them soon.

"I liked that group of girls. I see some real potential in some of them," I was telling Trinity as we walked from the hotel to our waiting limo.

"Yeah. I think Christy Schumer will—"

"Yo, Syn," someone called, interrupting Trinity. I looked around to see who had called me. There was a big black man in a cream-colored suit walking in my direction.

"You know him?" Trinity asked.

I studied the man's features as he walked toward us. He was black as night, no facial hair, and hair cut low. "I don't know."

When the man got closer, he flashed a smile. "Syn, what up, girl?"

It was then I realized he was actually a she. I couldn't believe my eyes. "Oh, my God! For real?"

"Who is he?" Trinity asked.

"He is a she," I said as I walked toward the stranger from my past. "Vega. What's up, girl?"

"Girl, I knew that was you. Look at you, lookin' like a big shot. I see you put that Boss Bitch concept to work," Vega said, looking me over like I was a super star. I was dressed modestly in a gray skirt suit and heels with my hair done up in a bun, but with the way Vega was staring at me, someone would've thought I was wearing the latest Versace dress.

"Nah, look at you with your expensive suit on. What are you doing in L.A.?" I asked as we embraced. Vega was still big, black, and ugly as ever, but she looked like she was living well.

"Business of L.A. is great. I have a place out here. Some of my girls work out here. You just contracted two of them: Christy Schumer and Anne Sessions."

I was surprised by the news. Christy and Anne didn't look like they swung that way. "Wow. Okay. So, what do you do?"

"I'm a manager," Vega smiled.

I knew that manager meant more than a representative. "Oh. Okay. Manager, huh? So, it looks like we're in business again, huh?"

"Yeah, yeah. We had some good times in Taycheeda, didn't we? Hopefully we can make a killing again," Vega smiled

"Well, look, I have to get going. Give me your number and maybe we can catch up sometime."

"Yeah. Let's do that. We can get together after I fly back from Milwaukee in a couple of days. I gotta meet with this nigga Calico back in the city. He wants a few girls."

I felt a chill run through my body when she said his name. "You know Calico?" I asked, trying not to let my hatred of him show in my demeanor.

"Shit, who don't know Calico? He a big fish in the Midwest. The Midwest is where Vega began. You gotta know a nigga like that to hit the big leagues. That nigga got long money."

I wasn't sure how I was going to do it, but I was going to use Vega to get to Calico. This was my break. "When did you say you would be back?" I asked, pulling out my cellphone.

"Couple days. Two at the most."

"Good. We need to discuss some business I think will benefit us both. What is your number?"

After getting Vega's number and promising to stay in touch, I walked back to my idling limo.

"That was a woman?" Trinity asked as I got in.

"Yeah."

"She looks like Biggie. Where do you know her from?"

"Let's just put it like this: she is someone from my past who showed up at just the right time," I smiled.

***

Vega was back in town two days later, and as promised, we got together. We were at my strip club. Den of Syn was making me a killing in L.A. Los Angeles was a bigger market than Milwaukee. It had a lot more people with a lot more money. Lots of sports figures and rappers stopped by to make it rain weekly.

"This is a nice club you got here, Syn. And your girls are… Whew! What would it take to get some of my girls up in here?" Vega asked as we looked out at the club from the V.I.P. booth.

"I'll tell you what. Since you are my girl, I'll see what I can do. Let me see the girls you have in mind and I'll get them in on a poppin' night. When the Miami Heat come to town, it's always poppin'."

When Vega smiled. I could see the dollar signs in her eyes. "I knew there was a reason I liked you, Syn."

"You scratch my back, and I'll scratch yours, Vega. You know how I get down. You put in a lot of work for me when we were locked up. If I can help you, you know I will."

"Look at you, Syn. Still got that Boss Bitch mentality. Just so you know, I stole some of your principles. I used to love listening to you kick that knowledge. You was a beast, girl."

After sharing a laugh. I decided we had spent enough time catching up. Now it was time to get down to business. "Yeah. Those were the days. So, how is business with Calico? How did you get a big player like him on your line, and how do I get in on the action?"

"So, that was the catch to lettin' my girls up in here, huh? You a slick bitch, Syn. But since you my girl, I'ma share the wealth. His money is long enough. Me and Calico been doing business for almost five years. A few years back I was featured in one of those 'G's Up, Hos Down' videos his media company produces. Then, one day I get a call from Calico talking about he wanna meet some

106

of my girls because he throwin' a party. Later that night, he rented ten of my girls. Gave me a grand for each one. The rest is history." I acted impressed. "Damn. He did it like that, huh?"

"Yep. He gets at me every month or so. He knew I keep them bad bitches on my team. He would probably like some of the girls you got up in here. I'll introduce y'all if you want."

"Um. Okay. But before you put me in bed with him, tell me more about y'all relationship."

"Not much to tell. Our relationship is strictly business. Try not to mix business and pleasure. We've met for lunch and dinner a few times, but that was for business. Boss Bitches keep business and personal lives separate," she smiled, quoting one of my lines.

"So, have you ever been to his house? Where does he live?"

"You can't just go knock on this nigga's door, Syn. He got security like the president. If you're not invited, you can't get in."

I had everything I needed. Now I needed to see if the bond we formed in prison was still tight. "Listen, Vega. I need to talk to you about something I don't ever want you to repeat."

"Okay. What's up?"

"I need you to get me close to Calico."

"Yeah. Sure. I told you that you have a few bitches up in here I think Calico would like to fuck with. He throws parties all the time. Always looking for some new girls."

"I'm not talking about my girls, Vega. I need you to get me close to Calico. So I can kill him."

Vega's eyes looked like they were about to pop out of her eye sockets. "Whoa, whoa, whoa! You want to kill Calico?"

"Yes. Him and the Hawaiian bodyguard."

"Berto? Wait, Syn. What the fuck is going on?"

I gave her the short version. "Calico got a hit out on me. Burned down my strip club and modeling agency in Milwaukee. My man is locked up with life for killing some of Calico's people, and the people Calico knows in prison are trying to get to my man. Neither one of us will be able to rest until his ass is dead."

Vega looked like I had just told her World War III was about to start. "Shit, Syn. You sure do know how to ruin a nigga's day," Vega said before becoming silent.

I remained silent, letting her think. She owed me. She was still alive because of me. And if she declined to help me, I was going to remind her that I stopped Rain from killing her.

"Syn, I gotta be honest, I don't want to do this. I'm not into this killer shit. I was in prison for robbery, not murder. But I do owe you. Shit, you saved my fucking life. I wouldn't be here today if it wasn't for you. I got your back, girl. What do you need me to do?"

On the inside I was doing back flips, but my exterior showed my game face. "It's simple. You get me close to him, and I'll do the rest. You don't have to get your hands dirty at all. Give me their information and tell me their weaknesses."

"Well, I'ma tell you right now that Calico will be hard to kill. If he has a weakness, I don't know what it is. He has bodyguards with him all the time, so it will be hard to get close to him. Plus, the streets saying he's at war with some niggas that call theyself the Trigga Klan, or something like that. So his people check and double-check everything and everyone he comes in contact with. Now, Berto will be easy. He lives alone and loves really dark-skinned girls. The darker, the better. He gets girls from me, too. All chocolate with toned bodies. You should probably try to get him first."

***

After my meeting with Vega, I went home feeling extra good. We had made plans to get the Hawaiian first, and then Calico. I already had Berto's address, and I had just the woman for the job: Jayda. She was as black as they came. I would have to give Calico's hit some more thought, but I would get to him. I didn't know how or when, but I was sure I would get to him.

After parking my orange Range Rover in the driveway, I let myself into the lavish house I shared with Trinity. The 8,000-

square-foot house, which I thought cost way too much, was in a gated community. Even though I didn't like the inflated price tag, there were a few things I did like about the pad – namely the pool and the fact the gated community had its own security. That made me feel safe. I knew that once I pulled behind those iron gates, neither Calico, nor anybody else for that matter, would be able to touch me unless they had a small army.

When I walked into the house, the first thing I noticed was Trinity. She was standing in the middle of the living room with her arms crossed. Her normally kept hair looked like a lion's mane, her light brown eyes looked like they were on fire, and she had an angry look on her face, like she wanted a confrontation. With me.

"Hey, Trinity. 'Sup?" I asked, dropping my keys into my purse and setting it on the end table.

"Hey, 'cousin,'" she spat, rolling her neck and staring me down.

I got a bad feeling. I didn't know how she found out, but she knew. "Hey, girl. You okay?"

"I don't know, 'Syncere.' Should I be?" She said my name the same way she said 'cousin.' She knew that was a lie, too. For some reason, I got mad.

"Trinity, what the hell is wrong with you? You got a issue, spit it out."

"Yeah, I got a problem, Loretta. I don't like being lied to."

Shit. There it was. My house of cards came crumbling down, and I was not prepared for the confrontation. So I said the only thing I could say. "I'm sorry, Trinity. I didn't know how to tell you."

"How about telling me the first time you came to my house instead of lying and saying you were my father's cousin? How could you lie to me about being my mother? Why would you lie?"

I wanted to reach out and hug her, but she looked like she might try to fight me if I touched her. "I'm sorry, Trinity. I didn't tell you because I didn't want you to be mad at me."

"What? Like I am now?"

"Yeah. Like you are now."

"I'm mad because you lied. All this time I've been having questions about my mom, and you've been right in front of me all along. You could've given me closure years ago, but you kept lying. You let me spend money I didn't need to spend to hire a private investigator when you could've just told me. Why, Loretta?"

"I didn't think you would understand. I thought you would be mad at me for leaving you. I thought you wouldn't want to talk to me."

"But you didn't give me a chance. So what if I would've gotten mad? That was my choice."

"I know. And I'm sorry."

"So, what else are you lying to me about, Loretta? Where have you been all my life, and why does Calico really want to kill you?"

As I searched my daughter's face, I knew any attempt to hide, lie, or deny anything would only do more damage to our relationship. She deserved to know the truth. Every painful bit of it. If she remained mad, like she said, that would be her choice. A choice I had to let her make.

"My real name is Loretta Jones, and I'm your mother. I wasn't there for you because I was in prison. I got locked up when you were six months old. I did seventeen years."

I paused, giving Trinity a chance to speak or ask questions. She didn't say anything, just stared at me, so I continued.

"I got locked up for killing my friend's boyfriend after he tried to rape me. I didn't think to call the police, so I grabbed you and ran. Plus, I wasn't really into calling the police since they had just killed your father. So, I went on the run. After a couple of months, I went to see my mother, and that's when the police arrested me. That was the last time I saw you until the day I came to your house and you and A.J. were fighting."

"I just can't believe you lied to me all this time. So, where is the rest of the family? My grandparents? My father's family?"

"I don't know where your father's family members are. After C-Money got locked up, they acted like they didn't know me. I couldn't even get them to buy you diapers. I was gonna raise you without their help. And my parents are dead. They died while I was in jail, in a car accident. You were in the car, too. Since we didn't have family in Wisconsin and I was in prison, they put you in the system. I'm sorry, Trinity. I am. I was a coward for not telling you who I was when we first met. If I could take it all back, I would. I just wanted to get to know you. I wanted to be there for you. I was trying to make things right, Trinity. I'm still trying."

"I don't know what to say to you, Syncere, or Loretta, or whatever your name is."

"C'mon Trinity. I'm Syncere. I'm still the same person."

"So, why did you change your name? Does this have anything to do with Calico?"

"No. I changed my name while I was in prison. The stuff with Calico started after I got out."

"So, why does he want to kill you."

"I took some money after I killed the man who tried to rape me. Turned out to be Calico's. When he found out I was out, he came to the club talking shit about me owing him some money. I didn't give it to him, so he tried to take my club and kill me. That's everything, Trinity. You know it all now."

We began a silent stare down. Her eyes showed anger and betrayal. My eyes pleaded for forgiveness.

"You should've told me this two years ago," she spat before walking away.

J-Blunt

Chapter 15

"See, Luke, this is exactly why the fuck I'm in the joint. 'Cause niggas like Gus wanna be on that robbin' shit. Them type of niggas don't know how to hustle, and they undercover haters. Thinkin' shit sweet. Then you gotta kill a nigga and end up in the joint, all because these niggas don't wanna go out and get they own," Li'l Dave vented.

I had met Li'l Dave a week ago when I started working in the welding shop as the janitor. Li'l Dave was light-skinned, stood about 5'7", 150 pounds, and had shoulder-length dreads. He was the welding shop tutor.

"Luke, you hear this bullshit?" Gus asked.

Gus was Dave's friend and debating partner. He was brown-skinned and about the same height and weight as Dave, but much younger. He was 21, but looked like he could still be in high school.

"Yeah, man. I hear him. He kinda got a point. I never hustled before, but I know the game," I added.

"C'mon, Luke. Don't be actin' naïve to the game. Robbin' is a hustle, too, just like sellin' dope. Shit been around before dope dealers. Niggas like Dave keep niggas like me in the strip clubs makin' it rain. You heard Lyfe Jennings. I be robbin' these niggas," Gus laughed.

All I could do was laugh. Being around these two was a riot. They kept me laughing at their crazy debates.

"Y'all are crazy. Are y'all, like, brothers or something?" C.O. Johnson, A.K.A. Tahiti, asked. She was sitting at her desk about twenty feet away from the workers' chilling area. She was the reason I had gotten the job, the reason I put up with the slave wages and manual labor. She was now a relief officer in the shop. Whenever the regular, Tom, was off, Tahiti filled in for him.

"If he was my little brother, I would've been whoopin' his ass," Dave laughed.

"Yeah. And then there woulda been another Kane and Able story," Gus shot back.

"Y'all are crazy," Tahiti laughed.

"Hey, Johnson!" our boss, Jack, a 25-year employee of the state called from across the shop.

"What's up, Jack?"

"I'm going to run up-stairs and talk to Karen. Can you handle the guys?"

"Yeah. They only have ten minutes till shop is over. I'll manage."

"Okay. You can let them leave a few minutes early if you want." Jack called as he left.

"All right, y'all. Shop is over. Come get y'all passes," Tahiti called.

The eight inmate students, along with myself, Gus, and Li'l Dave, lined up at her desk to get our passes. I made sure I was at the back of the line.

"Hey, Swanson. Hold on. I need you to help me move this gas tank," Tahiti said as she handed out passes.

I waited at her desk until she followed everyone to the door. When they left, she locked it. "We got about ten minutes," she said excitedly.

"Where?" I asked, ready to get it on. It had been two weeks since we had sex, and I was horny as hell. Our third shift rendezvous were sporadic since she worked wherever there was an opening, but now that we were in the welding shop, I was expecting to get pussy on a regular.

"In the bathroom."

As soon as we got in the bathroom, I started kissing her like I missed her. I threw her ass up on the sink and started pulling at her pants roughly.

"Oh, Luke! I like it rough," Tahiti moaned.

I was having a hard time getting her pants down. They were tight, and I couldn't get them past her wide hips. "C'mon, girl. Pull these mu'fuckas off."

She jumped off the sink and did a little shimmy dance, eventually pulling off one leg. That was good enough for me. I threw

114

her back up on that sink, spread her legs, and got on my knees. I hadn't eaten pussy in two years. I was about to tear it up!

"Ooh, Luke!" she moaned, rubbing my head as I attacked her pearl. I sucked the little hard ball like I was trying to suck sap out of a maple tree. It turned out I hadn't lost my cunnilingus skills. It didn't take her long to cum, and I was glad at that because my dick was harder than steel. When I got up from my knees, I pulled my pants down and dove in. I didn't know if it was because I wasn't getting sex like I used to, but I swore that Tahiti had some of the best pussy I had ever had. And I loved the way she moaned my name. It sounded like music.

"Oh yeah, Luke. Mm!."

My first nut came quick, but I didn't miss a beat. I figured I had about five minutes left, and I was going to use every second. I grabbed one of her legs and put it on my shoulder as I dug deeper.

"Oh, yeah. Shit! Mm, baby," Tahiti moaned, grabbing ahold of my shoulders.

I studied her face as I rammed her. Her eyes were closed, but her sex faces were beautiful. She looked caught between pleasure and pain. I could feel my second nut building. I lifted my head toward the ceiling, glancing in the mirror on the way up.

"Aw, shit!" I cursed, stopping my stroke.

Tahiti opened her eyes to see why I had stopped her painful pleasure. "Luke, baby, why… Aw, shit!"

We were busted. Jack had come back into the welding shop earlier than expected. Now we were all locked in an intense stare down.

"Jack. Um. Shit, man," I stuttered, staying inside of Tahiti. If he was going to report us, I was going to get my second nut.

"Jack, please don't say anything," Tahiti pleaded.

"Shit, I'm not going to say anything. I haven't gotten laid in two months. My wife has me in the doghouse. I was hoping you had room for one more."

The fear and worry that had spread across my face was replaced by a smile. Tahiti, however, didn't look so thrilled. "We ain't got a choice," I told her.

J-Blunt

"I know. C'mon, Jack," she whined.

"I knew there was a reason I liked you, Jack. Ever fucked a black girl before?" I asked as I stepped away from Tahiti and helped her off the sink.

"First time for everything," he grinned, grabbing at his pants.

"I can't believe I'm doing this shit," Tahiti laughed, spinning around and bending over.

I leaned against the sink and let her give me head while my boss hit it from the back. This was the first threesome I'd ever had with another man. It was both awkward and funny. The facial expressions Jack made while he fucked Tahiti had me dying on the inside. He looked like he was constipated.

"Ooh, yeah," Jack moaned, turning beet red as he came inside of Tahiti. "Wow. That was great. Now I understand the saying 'once you go black, you never go back,'" Jack cracked as he pulled up his pants.

"This stays between us, right?" I asked, guiding Tahiti's bobbing head.

"Yeah. Sure. You bet. Whatever you guys need, just let me know. By the way, you guys have to be out of here in about five minutes. I told Larry in maintenance he could bring his ladder in for repair."

"A'ight, Jack. Be done in two."

When Jack left, Tahiti stopped sucking me and went to lock the door. "I hate your ass, Luke."

"If by hate you mean love, then I hate your ass, too," I laughed.

"He nutted in me, Luke. That shit was nasty."

"I thought you was on the pill."

"I am, but I still didn't want an old white man nutting inside of me."

"Don't think about it like that, baby girl. What you did had to be done. You did a good job. We good now. Jack is on our team. But can we talk more about Jack later? I only got a couple minutes, and I need to get my second nut."

116

A Gangster's Syn 2

***

After leaving work, I got back to the cell hall just in time for afternoon count. This was where they literally counted every inmate in the prison, and if anyone was missing from their cells without a valid excuse, it would be hell to tell the captain. When the officer passed my cell, I grabbed a bar of soap and towel to do a quick wash-up in the sink. I had just finished toweling off when my cell door opened. The doors opened electronically, and there were no intercoms, so I had to walk down the four flights of stairs to see why my door had been opened.

"What's up?" I asked Sergeant Tolison.

"Swanson, you have an attorney visit."

During my walk to the visiting room, I thought about who had come to see me and why. The who part wasn't hard to figure out. It had to be my lawyer, Mike Thompson. But the why was puzzling. He normally sent me a letter or set it up for me to call through the social workers. Him popping up unannounced didn't sit right with me.

When I got to the visiting room. I gave my pass to the C.O. in the bubble and was made to wait for a couple of agonizing and stressful minutes. When they were ready for me, I was allowed to go into a small conference room behind the visiting room. Mike was inside waiting for me.

"Luke, how are you?" he asked, extending his hand. I shook it.

"Good. Good. 'Sup with you, man? What brings you here?" I asked, studying his face as I sat across from him at the small table. He wasn't wearing a smile, so I figured he wasn't bringing good news.

"I got a little bit of bad news for you, man. The circuit court denied you appeal."

It felt like the walls around me were closing in. "What? You serious?"

"Yeah, man. This is some bullshit, but this is where we are."

117

I could feel the anger building up inside of me. I wanted out. I wanted to go home. "I thought you said it was a good chance we would win? Thought you said the issue was solid?"

"That's just it, Luke. It was a chance. There is never really a guarantee. Judges are fickle."

"So, what now? That's it? I gotta spend the rest of my life in here?" I asked, starting to feel trapped.

"I will continue to fight for you, Luke. I know you were fucked over since the beginning of your case. You're not supposed to be in here. You should've gotten self defense."

"But what does all this mean? They denied us, man! These mu'fuckas don't want to let me go!" I yelled in frustration.

"Luke, this is a process, brotha. You have to let it run its course. I expected the trial court to deny you because no judge wants to admit he fucked up. The Court of Appeals is our next option. They are iffy, but they go by the letter of the law. If they deny us, then we go to the Wisconsin Supreme Court. You have a good issue, Luke. They have to rule on this. But I also have to tell you that The Supreme Court of Wisconsin only accepts about one out of every ten cases. However, if we have to go to them, I do feel that our case is strong enough to be accepted. If not, then we're on the United States Supreme Court. Just know I am fighting for you, Luke. I will not give up until you are free."

Chapter 16

"Luke, that's how these courts are, brah. They do this shit to ninety percent of the people that file an appeal. Don't nobody like admitting when they fuck up, especially these egotistical uber-righteous-ass judges. But don't let this shit throw you off yo' square. That judge's ruling was weak. He can't deny because of those old-ass statutes the D.A. used. You got a high profile case, and he just trynna save face. The court of appeals gon' overturn yo' shit, for sure."

As I listened to Big Ham's explanation, I started to feel a little better about my chances at being released in the near future. "Yeah, I hear you, Ham. I do. I just want all this shit to be over with. I was expecting to be going home on the first ruling. I'm tired of this prison shit. I can't help but think if I was white, I wouldn't even be going through this shit. I killed the nigga who shot me and ended up with life. That shit sounds crazy."

"Shit, you didn't know, nigga? Wisconsin is judicially the most racist state in the country. Look at all these niggas in Waupun and the rest of the prisons in Wisconsin. You mean to tell me that minorities commit more crimes than the majority race? Hell nah! It's systematic racism. How do we make up thirteen percent of the population but fifty percent of the prison popula-tion? Yeah, if you was white, you would be at home. That ain't no secret, nigga."

Big Ham and I became silent. During our moment of silence, I looked at the crowd of inmates we were walking in. We were all heading back to the unit from nighttime structured rec. There were thirty of us: seventeen black, eight Hispanic, four white, and one Asian. Based on this small group, it was clear racism was alive and breathing.

"Damn, I like that bitch," Big Ham mumbled, interrupting my thoughts.

I looked around to see who he was talking about. I spotted Tahiti about twenty yards away, heading in our direction. I immediately thought back to our sex-capade from that morning.

Ever since she gave Jack some pussy three days ago, he had been watching out for us while we snuck away and got it on. Just that morning I got to hit for a whole hour. I tore that ass up!

"Yeah. C.O. Johnson is the truth. That ass is like whoa!" I smiled.

"Man, Luke. I been locked up for seventeen years. If I got the chance, I would lick her from the rooty to the tooty, asshole and all."

"Big homie, it's official. You nasty," I laughed.

"Hey, Swanson," Tahiti smiled, giving me the eye as she walked past.

"Sup, Johnson," I nodded, remaining cool and acting nonchalant. Every inmate in the crowd turned to watch her walk to the back of our group to talk to our escorting officer.

"Damn, Luke! I see you got playa status," Big Ham cracked.

I didn't know how to respond. Big Ham was my boy, but I wasn't about to let him know I was fucking Tahiti. The less people who knew, the better. "Yeah. You know these broads know a real nigga when they see one," I laughed.

When we stopped at the metal detector, Tahiti eased her way closer to me. I made sure to shake Big Ham and be the last one through the machine. "What you doin' out here, girl?" I asked, keeping my voice low.

"I came to see you. I went to your cell, but you wasn't there. Wilson said you were at structured rec. I came to see if you keeping everything right for me and Syn. And I can see that you are," she smiled, looking me over.

"Girl, you crazy," I laughed, shaking my head and looking out over the crowd. There were about seven or eight prisoners looking at us. One in particular caught my eye. An older dude named Silk, whose cell was about five doors away from mines, was watching us extra close.

"You see that light-skinned nigga up there with the perm?" I asked, nodding toward Silk.

Tahiti followed my gaze. "You talking about Benson's old, freaky ass?"

"Yeah. Him. He all up in yo' shit. When he around, you gotta play it cool around me. I think he one of them old-school niggas that be hating if he can't get in on the action."

"Fuck Benson. I'll send his ass to the hole."

"Nah. Just lean back when he around. He good with that law shit and might try to pop some paper to get you investigated or moved around. I don't want that. I need you here with me."

"Aw, Luke! You feelin' me like that, huh? That's good, because I'm working third shift tonight. Don't be fallin' in love with me, boy. You know Syn ain't having that shit."

***

I woke up the next day to the sound of my phone vibrating. It was Syn. "Hey, baby. I thought we talked about you not calling my phone."

"I know. You were late with your call, so I figured I'd give you a ring. But I won't do it no more. Promise."

I checked my phone's face to see how late my call was. It was 6:08. I normally called every morning at 6:00 on the dot. "A'ight. I'ma give you a pass since I'm almost ten minutes late. So, what's up? How you doin'?"

"Fine. Guess what?"

"What?"

"I'm in Wisconsin. At my apartment. I flew in last night."

"For real? I thought you wasn't coming to town 'til next week."

"I decided to come early. When you told me about the appeal, I wanted to come then, but I had to wrap up some loose ends. But I'm here now."

"Yeah, that denial was pretty devastating. I want to come home so fucking bad. I just took Mike's words too literal. He said we had a good issue, and I thought I was going to get love right away. Now he's saying it's a process."

"Mike is right, baby. There is never really a 'for sure' when dealing with the courts. I tried self-defense, too. Rasheed's ass tried to rape me, but they didn't care. And they denied all of my appeals. But your case is different. They didn't put that lesser-included offense in the jury instruction. I believe Mike will get you out. I can't stop believing. I'm scared to stop believing."

"I hear you, baby. This shit is so frustrating. I can't do this shit for the rest of my life."

"And you won't have to, babe. You just have to have faith. Don't start giving up on me, Luke. I need you to be strong for us. Don't stop being my Superman."

The tenderness and sincerity in Syn's voice touched me. Sometimes, late at night when I was in my cell and the walls began closing in on me, I questioned her devotion. I had talked to plenty of dudes whose wives of five or ten years had left them high and dry, but here was this beautiful, powerful, headstrong, and damn near rich woman (whom I had only known for four months before I got locked up) doing all she could to keep me comfortable and encouraging me not to give up.

"You are amazing, you know that, girl?" I smiled, feeling like some of my burdens had been lifted.

"So are you."

"Okay. I'm back now. Thanks for the pep talk. I love you, girl."

"Good. Welcome back. And I love you, too."

"So, how are you and Trinity doing? She still mad at you?" I asked, switching subjects.

"She's coming around. Doesn't say much to me, though, but at least now we can be in the same room and work together."

"Give her some more time. She feels betrayed. You lied. She trusted you. The fact she hasn't moved out or quit her job means she doesn't hate you. She's just hurt, but she'll be okay."

"Yeah. I hope so. Besides you, she is my best friend, and I want my friend back. Wait. Somebody is at my door. I think it's Tahiti. She called me right before I called you." I listened as Syn and Tahiti greeted each other. "Okay, baby, I'm back. It's her."

"Ask Tahiti why she didn't speak to me before she left?"

I listened as Syn relayed my message. Then her and Tahiti started talking. It sounded like they were talking about Silk. I tried, but I couldn't hear all of their words.

"Luke, what the fuck is up with this nigga Silk?"

"Fuck, dude. I don't even want to think about his bitch-ass."

"Nah, baby. I think you need to hear this. Last night he asked Tahiti for some pussy. He told her he knows y'all are fucking, and he wants some pussy or some money."

A surge of anger filled my body. "What? You serious?"

"Yeah, baby. And she's a little shook up. She wanted to tell you last night, but she didn't want to wake you up because she knew he would be listening. That's why she didn't holler at you before she left."

"Shit. Old bitch-ass nigga," I mumbled before going silent.

"Luke?"

"Yeah, I'm still here. This is why I told her ass don't be pushing up on me when we out and about. These cats be haters."

"So, what do you want to do? Do you want to give him some money?"

"Hell nah! We ain't givin' his bitch-ass shit. We got breakfast in about ten minutes. This nigga ain't finna extort or blackmail us. If we give in, he gon' try this shit again. He only a couple cells down, so I'ma catch him in line."

"Luke, don't get in trouble over this, baby. I–"

"I'm good, Syn. Trust me. I'ma call you later. I gotta freshen up and hit this toilet. Love you, girl."

"Luke, wait. Don't you think we should talk about this some more?"

"I got it. Let me do this, Syn. I gotta go. Love you."

"I love you, too."

After brushing my teeth, washing my face, and using the bathroom, I threw on my state-issued green pants, a gray Hanes t-shirt, and by black high-top Nikes.

When the four buzzers rang signaling our tier was about to be let out for breakfast, I stood at the door, anxiously awaiting its opening. As soon as my door opened, I stepped out onto the range.

Silk was looking in my direction. As soon as we locked eyes, he turned around and began walking.

Coward-ass nigga!

I wanted to run up on him and chump-squeeze him, but I knew he was an old vet. Vets didn't scare easily, so I had to play it cool.

After descending the stairs, I mingled in with the rest of the inmates, keeping my eyes on Silk. He was only ten or so feet in front of me. I closed the distance quick, stepping on the heel of his shoe as we walked in the chow hall. He spun around to see who had stepped on his ankle.

"Oh, shit. My bad, Silk," I apologized, acting like it was an accident.

"Oh, what's up, Luke? How you doin' this morning, brotha?"

"I'm good. About to get up with these French toast."

"Yeah, yeah. Me, too. Hey, I wanted to holla at you about something," he said, pausing to look around. When he spoke again, it was a whisper. "What's up with you and Johnson? Is that you?"

I looked at him like he was speaking Russian. "What? Nah! You tripping, man. I wish."

"Nah, Luke. Check me out, playa. Dig. I see and hear everything that goes on around here, man, and I know you hit that. I heard y'all about a month ago. On third shift. I thought I was tripping at first, but I knew I heard some moans. And every time she work third shift, she always stop at yo' cell. I stuck my mirror out one time and seen her on her knees giving you head through the bars. So don't bullshit me, playa. I can help you or hurt you. I wanna help."

I looked around to see who was in earshot as we waited in line to get our trays from the server window. We were surrounded by inmates, but most of them were engaged in their own conversations and ignoring us. "Look, Silk, I don't know what you talking about, man. And I don't take kindly to threats. Let's leave this shit alone, alright?"

Silk gave me a long stare. The stare was followed by a sinister smile. "Luke, I been locked up for 23 years, and I ain't never going home. Since I been locked up, my momma and daddy died, and I don't got nobody looking out for me. The way I make my living is by lawsuits, helping these dudes in them courts, and by knowing who is doing what and when, and finding a way to get my hand in the pot. Luke, what you have is a gold mine that you may not know how to mine. I'm 53 years old. A fountain of wisdom is inside this head of mines. I'm not asking you for help, brotha. I need an opportunity."

Our turn up at the server window made me hold my response. I was glad at that because it gave me a few moments to calm down and think of a response. By the time we got to our table, I had cooled a bit and no longer wanted to punch him, but I did want to slap him still.

"Listen, Silk. I don't know you and you don't know me. We chopped it up about some law, but we don't know each other personally. And since we don't know each other that well, let me take this time to let you know that ain't nothing soft about me, and I don't like when somebody is trying to extort me. I don't know what you thought you saw, but it didn't have nothing to do with me."

Silk smiled at me as he took a bite of his French toast. "Luke, c'mon, young brotha. This is an opportunity. Have her bring me an ounce of coke and I'll forget about everything I seen. You got life, man. A clock with no numbers. You need that bitch for as long as you can keep her. I'd hate to see you lose something like that because you don't want to cut anotha black man in on the wealth. We are brothers. We supposed to stick together. One hand washes the other."

I no longer wanted to slap or punch Silk. I wanted to kill him. "Listen, Silk. I'ma tell you this one time. You ever threaten me again, I'ma fuck you up. I don't know what you talkin' about or what you think you saw."

Silk stopped chewing his food and began to stare at me. His stare was searching, like he was trying to read me, see how serious I was. Then he started laughing like I told a joke. "Luke, everybody knows you ain't no killa, man. The streets was talkin' 'bout you long before you got here. You locked up for shootin' some niggas over a bitch. Back in the day, we called niggas like you tender-dick niggas. Lettin' pussy move you a no-no. Do you realize you got life over a piece of pussy, and now you trynna have Johnson. Ain't you learned yo' lesson, man? Don't be threatenin' me over some pussy, baby boy. Let's eat together. Either that, or nobody won't be eatin' at all."

I was so mad I started to get the shakes. All I could do was clench my jaw and take deep breaths. I had no more words for Silk. He had mistaken me for something I wasn't and had even threatened me again. I knew I couldn't fight him. I had too much to lose. The fight would get me six months in the hole, and maybe an extra six months for my cellphone. And if he popped paper on Tahiti, I could lose her, too. So, I wasn't going to fight him. First chance I got, I was killing him.

"Luke, don't look so upset, brotha. Think of this as business. Take your emotions out. I'll give you some time to think about our proposition. By the way, I see you haven't touched your French toast. You gonna eat that?"

"Nah, Silk. You spoiled my appetite. That's all you."

When I got back to my cell, I couldn't stand still. I was beyond angry. In my mind, I was going over all the possible ways to kill Silk. I considered paying someone to do it, but I didn't trust anyone enough to even mention putting a hit out on someone. Plus, Silk was known. He had been in Waupun for fifteen years and knew lots of staff and inmates. The way I figured, the only way to get him done was to do it myself, and the only way I could get him and get away with it was to catch him in his cell. There were no cameras on the tiers. The problem would be catching him with his door open when no one was around.

The hit would have to be spontaneous.

I ended up pacing my cell until it was time for me to go to work. My cell door opened up at eight o'clock on the dot.

After gathering my wooden shank and cell phone, I left the cell. I had just closed my door when I noticed that Silk's door was

126

open. Everything I thought about while pacing my cell came flooding back to my mind. I looked up and down the range to see what doors were open. The only doors that looked to be open were mine and his. I knew this was an opportunity I couldn't pass up. He needed to die. Right now.

I pulled my shank as I crept toward his door. During my creep, I looked in every cell along the way to check on the occupants. It was still early, so the guys in all four cells between us were asleep. When I got to Silk's door, I stopped to take a peek inside. He had his back to me, putting on his shoes. I could feel my adrenaline surge. My pulse thundered loud in my ears. I knew it was now or never. I chose now.

Silk never seen me coming. I ran up behind him, put my hand over his mouth, and shoved my shank into his Adams Apple.

Silk thrashed around, trying to break free from my grip. I held on tight and drove the shank deeper into his neck. A few moments later, his thrashing calmed and his body went limp. I dropped him on the bed and surveyed the damage. Blood was everywhere, all over my hands and shirt, on the floor, some on the wall, and it covered Silk from his chin to his shoes. The sight of all the blood mortified and excited me. I had killed a man with my bare hands. It felt primal and animalistic.

As I looked around, I knew I couldn't leave his cell covered in blood. I took off my shirt and wiped the blood from my arms and hands. When I was sure that all the visible blood was gone, I grabbed one of Silk's shirts from his clothesline and put it on. Then I used my bloodied shirt to grip my shank and snatch it from his neck. A stream of blood flew across the room, splashing the wall. After wrapping the shank in my bloody shirt, I tucked all the evidence in the front of my waist and closed Silk's door on the way out.

I maintained a cool stroll as I descended the stairs and grabbed my pass for the officer's desk. I made sure to grab Silk's pass too, crumpling it in my fist. If the C.O.s had seen his pass, they would wonder why he hadn't come down and probably go check on him. I didn't need that. I needed to buy as much time as I could to get out of the cell hall and off to work. I needed to get out of these clothes and in the shower.

"Luke! 'Sup, nigga?" Gus called as soon as I walked in the shop.

"Gus, what it do, homie?" I smiled, giving him a fist bump.

After greeting the rest of my co-workers, boss, and C.O. Tom, I headed to the supply closet to get some cleaning supplies. My next stop was the clothing cabinet to grab a set of well-worn shop clothes. After gathering all my things, I went to the inmate bathroom to take a shower. When done, I used the supplies to clean the shower. After cleaning the shower, I took my clothes, cell phone, and shank over to one of the stick welding booths. I dressed in a leather overcoat, gloves, helmet, and goggles, then went in the booth to set everything on fire.

I hated burning the cellphone, but I had to do it. I knew once they found Silk's body, we would be put on lockdown. I couldn't risk the phone getting caught up. The call logs would lead them right to me.

When everything was consumed by fire and turned to ash, I breathed a sigh of relief and went to do my work.

I had just finished cleaning Jack's office when all hell broke loose. A loud alarm went off, radios began blaring out commands, and the telephones began ringing.

"All inmates report back to their units. The institution is now under a lockdown!"

Chapter 17

"C'mon, Jayda. You know you could've called Trinity and had her approve the payment for the cases of Smoke Liqueur. I'm already at Waupun, and I need to see my baby."

"Luke can wait a few more minutes, Syn. Damn."

"He's not the one that can't wait. I ain't seen my man in two weeks. I need to get in there."

"I just need you to know I'm about to give this dude an $8,000 check. Your mini-me is still tripping. She still hasn't forgiven me for not telling her your secret that I never knew. So, if at all possible, I'm dealing with you. Hell, I still can't believe she's your daughter. I mean, I should've known because she looks and acts just like you, but I just never figured you to be the motherly, maternal type."

"Yeah, yeah, yeah. Heard it all before. Just give the man the check and get the cases. Is that all you want?" I asked, ready to end the call. Jayda was wasting my time, and I was ready to go. I wanted to taste Luke's lips and feel his hard body pressed against mines.

"Damn, Syn. You not about to get no dick, bitch. I—"

After hanging up the phone, I flipped down the driver's side visor to give myself a once-over in the mirror. Eyelashes were good. The little blush on my cheeks had them rosy. Luke's favorite lip-gloss, cotton candy, had my lips shiny and soft. I looked devilish, just how he liked it.

I hopped out of my Kia and took the time to adjust my skintight black leather pants to make sure they were hugging my ass just right. Luke loved when I wore tight pants, and I couldn't wait to see his reaction when he seen my ass in these.

As I walked toward the huge iron gate that separated my man from the free world, I noticed there were only four cars parked outside the prison. I thought that was strange. There were normally ten to fifteen cars parked out front. Then, when I got to the gate's entrance, I found out the reason for so few cars. The gate was locked, and there was a sign attached to it.

THE INSTITUTION IS UNDER A LOCKDOWN
VISITS WILL BE HALTED UNTIL
LOCKDOWN IS OVER

"What the fuck?" I cursed, rattling the gate and hoping this was some kind of misunderstanding.

"This prison is under lockdown, ma'am."

The voice came from my left. I looked toward the 30-foot-high gun tower and seen a correctional officer leaning on the railing.

"What? Why? For how long?"

"Don't know why. Don't know how long. Sorry." He didn't look sorry.

"How can I find out when the lockdown will be over?"

"Whoever you came to see will have to contact you. Either that, or you can call and check in with the front office during normal business hours."

I got a strange feeling in my gut. Somehow I knew the lockdown had something to do with Luke. When I got back in my SUV, the first number I dialed was Tahiti's.

"Hello?"

I could hear the sleep in her voice, but I didn't care. "Why didn't you tell me the prison was on lockdown?"

"What? What are you talking about, Syn?"

"I'm sitting in my truck in front of Waupun. I tried to go visit Luke, but they won't let me in. They said the prison is on lockdown."

That woke her ass up. "What? For real? I don't know, Syn. Do you think it has something to do with Luke?"

"That's what I need you to find out. This is what I'm paying you for."

"Okay. I'm woke. I'm gonna make some calls. Let me call you back."

After I hung up, I drove back to my apartment. I had just closed the door behind me when my phone rang. It was Tahiti. "What did you find out?"

"Somebody got killed."

I immediately thought about Luke and Silk. "Who was it?"

"I don't know. Everybody is tight-lipped. Information is being given out on a need-to-know basis, but it did happen in the southwest cell hall. That's where Luke is."

Shit!

"Syn, you there?"

"Yeah. I'm here."

"Do you think Luke–"

"No! And don't you say it or even think it! What all do you know? How long will they be on lockdown?"

"I don't know. Trish said indefinitely. My guess is a month. Maybe two. They have homicide detectives investigating."

Double shit!

"Okay. Um, I have to get some things in order. I'ma let you go. Are you going into work today?"

"Yeah. I go in at two."

"Good. Try to talk to Luke and see how he is doing. Tell him to call me when he can. And keep me posted on who got killed."

"Okay. I got you, girl."

After hanging up with Tahiti, I ignored Luke's warning and called his phone. It went right to voicemail.

"Luke, this is your wifey. I'm worried about you, baby. Give me a call as soon as you can. I love you so much. Please call me."

After leaving the message, I threw my phone on the couch and started pacing the living room. Luke had killed Silk. I could feel it. He had changed. The killings had changed him, and prison was changing him even more. I just hoped he was careful enough not to get caught. he already had one homicide. He did not need another one. Not when he was still appealing his case.

I paced my living room for 45 minutes, trying to decide my next move. I couldn't talk to Luke, couldn't help him, and would have to wait for him to reach out to me through Tahiti or whenever they let him use the phone. I realized I would probably go crazy if I stayed in Waupun. I needed to go.

I grabbed my phone and booked a flight home. The next plane to California left Milwaukee in four hours. Even though Milwaukee was only forty-five minutes from Waupun, I decided to start my trek early.

During my drive, I gave Trinity a call. "What?" she answered dryly.

"Well, hey to you, too. You sound happy to hear from me."

"Not funny. What do you want, Syn?"

"I want you to throw out that attitude and meet me at the airport. My plane leaves in four hours."

"You coming home?"

"Yeah. They got the prison on lockdown."

"Okay. I'll be there."

"And you need to—"

Click.

"Hello? Trinity? I know this heffa didn't hang up on me," I mumbled, looking at the screen on my phone to see the call had ended. "Little bitch," I mumbled before tossing my phone on the passenger seat.

***

I checked my watch as I disembarked the airplane. It was a little after one in the morning. The jet lag had kicked my ass, and I couldn't wait to get in the passenger seat of Trinity's Benz. I was going to sleep on the ride home, and then run and swan dive into my bed and sleep some more.

I looked around for Trinity as I walked through the terminal. I looked around for about five minutes before deciding to check by the front doors. Still no sign of Trinity, and her car wasn't parked out front. I gave her cell phone a try. No answer. As I stood there looking up and down the row of parked cars, I realized Trinity had stood me up. I was pissed. I couldn't believe she didn't show up to get me after everything I had done for her. Not only was I her

132

mother, but I was also her boss. Nobody leaves their boss high and dry.

I hopped in one of the cabs that was parked at the curb and got a ride home. The entire ride I thought about how I was going to kick her ass. When the cab pulled up to my house, I seen Trinity's Benz parked in the driveway. No lights were on in the house. There was no emergency, no reason for her not to pick me up from the airport. From the looks of it, she stood me up to catch up on sleep. That got me even madder.

After letting myself in the house, I went right to Trinity's room. I busted open the door and hit the light switch. "You still want to play these childish-ass games, Trinity?"

Her and her boyfriend, Myron, shot up in bed like the FBI had kicked in their door. "Oh. I'm sorry, Syn. I forgot," she said nonchalantly.

I waited to see if she had more to say. She didn't, and she didn't look sorry at all. "Sorry? You left me hanging, and all you have to say is sorry?" I screamed, wanting to crawl across the bed and slap her in the face.

"Please, Syn. It ain't even like that. I forgot to pick you up from the airport. Sorry. It's not a big deal. You're here now. It's not like I forgot to tell you I was your mother."

Oh, no she didn't! And she had the nerve to roll her eyes.

"Look, Trinity, I told your ass I was sorry. Either you gon' get over it or you're not, but what you not about to do is throw me not telling you that I am your mother in my face every time you get mad or fuck up. I'm not only your mother, but I'm also the only family you got, and I'm your boss. You work for me. If I tell your ass to pick me up, you better be there or start looking for a job and a place to stay. I've done everything for you since I found you. I gave you a job, a place to stay, stability and security. When I met you, A.J. was kicking your ass and you were struggling to make ends meet. You don't worry about none of that shit no more. Why? Because of me. Yeah, I lied about being your mother, but you need to get over it. You're twenty years old, not two."

Trinity looked at me like she was about to cry. Myron looked caught between conflicting thoughts of defending his girlfriend or leaving the room. He chose his best option and kept his ass silent.

"Okay, Syn," Trinity mumbled, crossing her arms and avoiding eye contact with me.

I wasn't satisfied with her response. I didn't like her body language. Plus, I needed to let her know there would only be one Boss Bitch in this family. "Okay what?"

Trinity gave me a 'you gotta be kidding me' look. I stared harder, letting her know I was serious.

"We good, Syncere. We have an understanding. I will get over you not telling me you're my mom. And I won't throw it in your face no more."

"And?"

She looked at me with a question in her eyes.

"Airport."

After a deep sigh, she mumbled, "And I'm sorry for leaving you at the airport. It won't happen again."

"Damn right it won't happen again, or else you—"

I was cut off by the vibrating inside my purse. I pulled out my phone and seen it was Tahiti. I pushed my issue with Trinity to the back burner as I answered. "Hey, girl. Is everything okay with Luke?"

"Did you get my voicemail messages? Why didn't you call me back?"

"What? No, I haven't checked my messages. I was on the plane, and I cut off my phone. What's up? How is Luke?"

"He's okay. He doesn't have his phone, though. He said he had to throw it away before they went on lockdown."

"Okay. I'll get him another one. So, who did they say got killed?"

"Steven Benson."

I tried to place the name. I couldn't. "Who is he? Should I know who that is?"

"It's Silk."

It felt like I had been punched in the chest. I hoped to God Luke had got someone to kill him and hadn't done it himself.

"Syncere? What's going on? Is Luke okay?" Trinity asked, pulling me from my thoughts. I looked up and seen her and Myron all in my face.

Instead of answering her, I left her room, heading for mine. "What happened, Tahiti?"

"All I know is they found him dead in his cell. He got stabbed. The detectives are interviewing everybody in the cell hall. Even Luke."

J-Blunt

Chapter 18

One Month Later

"C'mon, Swanson. Let's get this pat down over with so you can get in there and see your girl! She's looking good, too," C.O. Klien joked as he pulled on a pair of blue latex gloves.

"You the one movin' slow. Let's go, Klien," I said, kicking off my shoes and spreading my arms east and west. I knew the procedure. I had been on hundreds of visits. Pat searches were standard procedure for all inmates entering the visiting room.

"You in the southwest cell hall?" he asked as he gave me a quick pat down.

"Yeah. Been trying to get out the southwest cell hall, but I guess I got caught up in the red tape. Then this lock down for the last month got everything fucked up."

"Who you telling? We had to make all of your meals. I get paid to watch you guys, not do physical labor. If I have to put mayo on one more sandwich, I'm going to retire."

"Good thing the lockdown is over. I was tired of eating cold cut sandwiches three times a day."

After leaving the search area, I grabbed my paper pass, heading toward the visiting room. I couldn't wait to see Syn. Being on lockdown had deprived me of visits and my sex-capades with Tahiti. It had been a little over a month since I last touched a woman. I couldn't wait to touch, smell, and kiss Syn.

When I opened the door to the visiting room, I began looking for Syn. It didn't take long to find her. She stood out like a doe in a pack of lions.

"Mm-mm-mm! Look at you, girl!" I smiled, stopping to take all of her in as she walked toward me. Even though my girl was almost 40 years old, she was crushing most 20-year-olds with her body and looks, including slightly slanted brown eyes, juicy lips, honey-colored skin, and a body that would make the Pope lust. She packaged her goodies in white leather pants, a black sheer blouse, and pink high heels. Her hair was done up in long, flowing curls. If I didn't know her and had passed her on the street, I would've sworn she was somebody famous.

"Hey, baby," she squealed, trotting toward me with open arms.

"Damn, girl. You look so mu'fuckin' sexy. I gotta get up outta here," I groaned as I took her into my arms. She looked, smelled, and felt good. She reminded me of home.

"Ooh, Luke. You feel so good, baby," she moaned before reaching up to kiss me.

"Damn, girl. I missed yo' ass so much," I managed, leading her toward our table after we came up for air.

"Me too. Not being able to hear your voice was like a life sentence. When you called me yesterday, it felt like I won the lottery."

"Hell yeah. And you did a good job keeping up with the mail. I'm surprised you had time to write so many letters."

"I made time. I told you I got you, baby. I don't care how many letters I have to write or how much money I have to spend on plane tickets. I got your back, baby. I need you in my life. You sacrificed everything by staying with me and getting involved in my drama. I won't ever forget that, baby. I'm going to ride this out with you, no matter how long it takes."

"Damn, woman. You sure know how to leave a nigga speechless. I think we both hit the lottery with each other."

"We did. Cha-ching!" Syn cracked. After we shared a laugh, Syn became serious. "So, how are you doing? Is everything okay? Are you okay?"

I knew she wasn't asking about my mental or physical health. She wanted to know about Silk. I hadn't wrote about it in our letters because I wasn't sure if they were monitoring our mail. "I'm good. Had all my ducks in a row."

"What about the detectives? Have they talked to you?"

"Yeah. They talked to everybody in our cell hall. They talked to everybody that live on our tier twice. They know I went to work at eight o'clock, but so did about 75 other inmates. Ain't no cameras on the ranges. No witnesses. No evidence."

138

A look of relief spread across Syn's face. "Whew! I was so worried about you, baby. But the next time you get in some shit, how about we just pay somebody to do the dirty work? You can't be gettin' your hands dirty. I need you at home."

"I hear you, baby. I do. Just know I will do anything to protect us."

"Aw, baby. I like it when you be Superman," Syn gushed.

"You crazy, girl," I laughed.

"Oh. I forgot to tell you, I found a house in Fox Lake. I'm having Tahiti handle everything. It's going to cost a pretty penny, but I think it's worth it. Don't gotta worry about no more nosy neighbors because it's on a half acre of land. Me and Tahiti can make as much noise as we want."

A visual of Tahiti and Syn getting it on flashed in my mind. "She moving in with you?"

"You better believe it. I need her to keep the house while I'm in L.A."

***

After my visit with Syn, I made it back to the cell hall just in time for rec. I planned to hit the weights extra hard today. I was still stressing about the detectives questioning me twice. Even though I knew there was no way for them to link me to his death, the what-ifs still stressed me a little bit. Nothing was for sure nowadays, and I was going to use the uncertainty to make me go harder.

After grabbing my shank, a change of clothes, some towels and soap, I left for rec. The recreation area, or 'Big Top', was about the size of a full-sized YMCA gym. A full-length basketball court, two handball courts, a weight lifting area, and about twenty tables for board games filled the space. A bathroom and shower area was off to the side, next to the weight piles.

"C'mon, Big Ham. Go all the way down with that shit. Don't cheat me out my money!" I encouraged as I stood over him, spotting him on the bench press. He was on his eighth rep, pressing about 300 pounds.

"Nine. Urgh! Ten!" he yelled, finishing his set.

When he got up from the bench, I was about to get down, but stopped when I seen Money, Buck, and three other dudes headed in our direction. I knew they were up to no good. "You see this shit?"

Big Ham turned to see what I was talking about. "Yep. Ay, Aqui?" Big Ham called to one of his Muslim brothers.

"Sup, brah?" Dark Man answered, pausing in the middle of his set of curls. Dark Man was dark-skinned, about 6' tall, weighed about 230 pounds, and wore his hair in cornrows to the back.

"You see these jokers?" Big Ham asked, nodding toward Buck and company.

"Yep. Ay, Mill? Look up," Dark Man said, getting the attention of another Muslim brother. His name was Jamil. He was short and dark-skinned with a muscular upper body and little legs.

"Oh, yeah. Who got pokes?" Jamil asked, immediately getting on point.

"I do," I answered.

"Me too," Dark Man chimed in.

"I like our odds," Jamil smiled.

While my boys sized up our potential rivals, I looked around for guards. There were four of them. They were looking toward the basketball court as that's where most of the action was taking place, but there were cameras. Several of them. And one of them was pointed right at us. I thought about what Syn said about paying someone to put in work for me. That advice was good, but right now I wasn't in a position to heed it. Money and his gang wanted problems, and I couldn't back down. Not now, not ever.

"What up, fam? Can we get in wit' ch'all?" Buck asked as they closed the distance between us.

"Nah," I said firmly, giving them all mean mugs.

"Y'all ain't got no monopoly on this shit," Money said and walked over to adjust the weight.

Big Ham snatched the weight pin from his hand. "Move, nigga. We got this."

Money swung first, and then the whole gym went up. While Ham and Money fought, Jamil, Dark Man, and I went at the others. I ended up knuckling up with a tall, light-skinned dude with long braids and platinum teeth. We squared up, and I wasted no time getting to work. I ran at him, swinging a combination of punches. I landed all of them to his face. He fell like a sack of potatoes.

"Break it up!" I heard C.O.s yell.

I ignored them and turned my attention to Big Ham. He was over by the bench press fighting Money and one of the dudes who came with him. I pulled out my shank and ran for Money. I was about to silence his ass once and for all.

Money spotted me before I could get to him. When he seen the wooden shank in my fist, he tried to run and ended up tripping over the weight bench. By the time he got back to his feet, I was upon him.

"Ah!" he screamed, jerking away after I drove the shank into his upper back. He spun around to face me, a terrified look in his eyes. I approached him slowly. Every time he took a step back, I took a step forward. Stabbing him had sent a surge of adrenaline through my body. I wanted him to die with his eyes open. I wanted him to know I killed him, so I began taunting him.

"I knew you was a bitch, Money. I'ma tell Calico how yo' ass was screaming like– Ah, shit!" I yelled, grabbing at my side as a sharp pain ran through my body. Somebody had stabbed me!

I spun around just in time to see Buck driving his blood-coated metal shank toward my stomach. I tried to block it, but couldn't. "Ah, shit!" I yelled, dropping my shank as I fell to my knees. I grabbed at my wounds. I could feel the blood oozing from my body. It hurt like hell, and my torso felt like it was on fire.

I ended up on my butt, using my feet to scoot away from Buck. I wasn't moving fast enough. He kept coming toward me with the shank, a bloodlust look in his eyes.

When he was almost upon me, Big Ham appeared behind him with my shank in his hand. He drove it in the side of Buck's neck. Buck's eyes bulged like they were about to pop out of his head. He grabbed at the wooden shiv lodged deep into his neck as he fell to the floor.

I tried to stand to my feet. It was tough, but with the help of the wall, I managed to stand. That's when I heard three loud pops. It sounded like gunshots.

I looked across the gym and seen smoking canisters of gas flying through the air. One of them landed about ten feet away from me.

The tear gas came out.

Tears blurred my vision as the choking began.

Chapter 19

"Stay with me, Jayda. All I need you to do is get in there and make sure he leaves the door unlocked. As soon as I get in, you can leave."

Jayda looked over at me with tears in her eyes. She was beyond scared. I hated to see my friend like this and wished I had someone to replace her, but I didn't, so she would have to go through with the plan.

"I'm nervous, Syn. I don't know if I can do this."

"We already talked about this, Jayda. I need you, girl. My family needs you. Don't fold on me now. We're here. If I don't get to him, he will kill me."

"But I'm scared," she whined.

"C'mon, Jayda. I need you to soldier up. We Boss Bitches. I have to do this. I've always had your back, now have mines. Please." I hated begging, but if that meant she would get her ass out of this van and into the house, then I would get my Keith Sweat on. This was a golden opportunity. I couldn't let it slip through my grasp.

"Okay. I'll do it," Jayda agreed, still looking nervous.

"That's my girl. Now, get yo' fine ass in that house and tempt his ass," I said, giving her naked thigh a slap.

Jayda was dressed in a light blue mini-skirt and a see-through white blouse that left nothing to the imagination. Her Hershey-dark skin was flawless, and her athletic body looked tight. She was almost forty, but her body looked twenty.

When she climbed out of the mini van, I watched her through the sliding door's tinted window. She walked up the walkway of the white townhouse and stood on the stoop. She looked back at the van one last time before ringing the doorbell. The door opened a couple seconds later and she walked in.

Part one of the mission had been accomplished. In three minutes I was going to pop in and exact my vengeance.

And that's when my phone began vibrating. I checked the number. It was Tahiti. I thought about letting my voicemail pick it up, but I didn't. Something told me to answer.

"Hello?"

"Syn, Luke is in the hospital!" Tahiti yelled.

I didn't think I heard her right. It had to be a mistake. "What? What are you talking about? I just seen him a couple of hours ago."

"I'm not playing, Syn. Luke is in the hospital, for real. It's bad."

It felt like the whole world had just gone dark. "Where is he? What happened?"

"There was a fight at rec. He got stabbed. The institution is on lockdown, again. I just found out he was involved. They're not telling us much, just that a few inmates got stabbed and one of them died."

I went into full panic mode. "No, no, no, Tahiti! I paid your ass to watch him. How the fuck did this happen?"

"It happened at rec. That's not my post."

"So, where is he now? Is he okay?"

"They took him to a hospital in Madison. You won't be able to see him. He's under armed guard and in critical condition."

Hearing that he was in critical condition almost gave me a nervous breakdown. "What? No, Tahiti. No. Not right now. Shit!"

"I'm sorry, Syn, but there ain't nothing I can do right now."

It felt like I was in a nightmare. Right when I was on the verge of getting my payback, Luke gets stabbed.

"Syn, I don't have much time to talk, but there is one more thing."

I knew she was about to drop a bomb. "What?"

"There is a tape. They record everything around here. I haven't seen it yet, but I know they have it. If Luke was in the riot, they'll probably try to charge him with party to a crime for the murder. He—"

"Get that motherfucking tape, Tahiti! You hear me? Get that fucking tape! He is still appealing his case and might be coming home soon. Get that damn tape, Tahiti!" I screamed.

"I will try. It's up in control, and I don't have access right now. The police are here, but I don't know if they've seen it yet."

"Tahiti, I don't care what you have to do. Just get that damn tape!"

"Okay. I will. I promise. I have to go. Somebody is coming."

I sat in the van, stunned. I couldn't believe Luke had been stabbed. Now he was in the hospital in critical condition, and there was a tape. My heart was heavy with worry about my man. Why did it have to happen now, right when I was on the verge of getting revenge? I wondered if it was some kind of payback for him killing Silk? Luke told me he carried a shank. I wondered if he killed the person who stabbed him. If it was on tape, I wondered if that meant he could get self-defense? I didn't need him to get charged with another murder. If he did, there was no way possible for him to come home, no matter what happened with his appeal.

I don't know how long I sat in that van thinking about Luke, but at some point Jayda crossed my mind. She was in the house with Berto. Shit!

I snapped into action and emerged from the van. I looked up and down the block as I walked toward the house. The block was empty, and the sun was just going down. Everything looked good, and the coast was clear. When I got to the porch, I gave myself a look-over. I had on all-black everything: black long sleeve t-shirt, black jeans, black Nikes, and black gloves.

When I tried the door, it opened. Jayda had done good. I opened the door slowly, pulling the silenced .22 caliber Berretta from my pocket as I crept into the house. The living room was quiet and empty. After closing the door, I looked around and listened for movement. Berto's house was a typical bachelor pad. Big TV, stereo system, thick blue carpet, and black leather furniture. I was thankful for the carpet. It meant he wouldn't hear me creeping.

J-Blunt

After taking in my surroundings, I tiptoed across the living room and toward the hall. I heard voices coming from one of the rooms. I kept the pistol high as I walked slowly down the hall. When I got to the room where the voices were coming from, I paused outside the door. I could hear Jayda laughing. I peeked in the room and seen them on the bed. Berto was sitting in the middle of the bed, Jayda was straddling his lap. The front of her blouse was open, and he was sucking her breasts.

"Pay back is a bitch, ain't it, Berto?"

When Berto looked up, he was staring down the barrel of my silenced pistol. He stopped fondling Jayda and gave me all of his attention. I could've sworn I seen a smile spread across his face.

"I knew I seen this bitch before," he said, wrapping an arm around Jayda.

Jayda tried to move, but he wouldn't let her go. Berto had muscles upon muscles. I knew Jayda wasn't getting out of his grasp if he didn't want her to.

"Let her go," I ordered, stepping further into the room.

"I'm not dying by myself, Syn," he said, ducking behind Jayda and using her for a shield.

I side-stepped to get a better angle. Berto was ready for that. He jumped out of the bed like lightning, taking Jayda with him. He stood with her in front of him, wrapping his arms around her neck and face.

"Put the gun down or I'ma break her neck."

I could see the fear in Jayda's eyes as Berto applied pressure to her throat. As I looked into her eyes, I hated myself for getting her involved, but I wasn't dropping my gun. Berto would kill us both if I did.

"Let her go, Berto. This is between us," I said, trying to flank him. He shifted again, keeping Jayda between us.

"Hell nah. This bitch is in this, too. Bitch set me up. Now, you got three seconds to drop that gun or I'm snapping her shit."

Jayda gasped and her eyes bulged as he applied more pressure to her throat. Her eyes pleaded for me to help her.

I knew I couldn't. Berto wasn't going to let her go. I had to make a decision. I had no choice.

So I shot her.

The bullet made a slapping sound as it dug into her forehead. Jayda continued staring at me as the life drained from her eyes.

Berto looked surprised that I had shot her. When he realized he no longer had a hostage, he dropped Jayda and charged at me. I squeezed the trigger as fast as I could. I watched as my bullets tore into his face, chest, and stomach.

It took ten of my bullets to drop the muscle-bound Hawaiian. When he fell at my feet, I turned and ran from the house. I didn't start crying until I got in the van and pulled away.

I hated having to kill my friend, but I didn't have a choice. Once Berto got his hands on her, she was as good as dead. He wasn't going to die alone. And he didn't.

J-Blunt

Chapter 20

"Good afternoon, Mr. Swanson. How are you feeling today?"
I opened my eyes and seen a thick, brown-haired white woman wearing purple nurse scrubs standing at the foot of my bed. She was reading my vital chart hanging from the footboard.

"Okay, I guess. My body hurts and I'm still locked up, but I'm alive, so…"

"Could be worse."

"How? I'm chained to a bed with 35 stitches in my stomach and back."

"Try to be optimistic, Mr. Swanson. You have your life. That is a blessing. Do you mind if I check your bandages?"

"Nah," I mumbled, using my free hand to lift my shirt.

After examining the gauze on my stomach, she helped me sit up so she could check my back wound. Sitting up hurt like hell. It felt like somebody was burning me on my stomach with a hot welding torch.

"You are healing nicely. A couple more days and we'll be releasing you."

"Great. I like the overtime, but this place is boring. No offense, ma'am." C.O. Jamison spoke up from his seat by the window. He was one of my babysitters. His counterpart, C.O. Brovlowski, had his eyes glued to the afternoon news program on TV.

"I understand, officer. Mr. Swanson, give us a call if you need anything," the nurse smiled politely before leaving the room.

"Damn, Jamison. You sure know how to chase women away," I cracked.

"Aw, she was busted, anyway. Did you see how fat her ass was? Nobody wants that shit. It's all loose and jiggly. I like a tight ass. One you can bounce a quarter off."

"C'mon, man. You sound crazy. Them little muscular booties is played out. It's all about big booties and twerkin'. Didn't Miley Cyrus teach you anything?"

"Now, that's a good ass. Not too big and not too small. Just right," Brovlowski chimed in.

All I could do was shake my head. I was about to tell Brovlowski to change the channel when my room door opened up. I looked up and seen another officer, C.O. Washington, walking into the room. He was followed by Tahiti. My eyes lit up when I seen her.

"Hey, guys. What's up? Second shift time," C.O. Washington said.

"About time. I need a beer," Jamison said as he got up and stretched.

"Hey, Swanson. You been causing trouble?" Tahiti asked, smiling at me and lickin' her lips.

I was happy as hell to see her, but I kept my composure. "C'mon, Johnson. You know I don't cause no trouble. I'm a peaceful man."

"Says the guy laid up in the hospital with two shank wounds," Brovlowski cracked as he and Jamison headed for the door.

"It was all a misunderstanding."

When Jamison and Brovlowski left, Washington got my attention. "Listen, Swanson. We're both new to this hospital guard shit, so you're going to have to bear with us. We won't cause you any problems if you won't cause them for us. Cool?"

I looked back and forth from him to Tahiti. She had a look in her eyes that let me know she was in control.

"I'm fucked up, Washington. I ain't trynna cause no trouble. I don't wanna have to go back to Waupun before I'm ready. I want to enjoy this cable TV for as long as I can. Feel me?"

"Hell yeah, I feel you. What's on ESPN?" he asked, walking over to change the channel.

"Man, they still talking about Hunt. I'm tired of hearing about that shit. He beat up a girl. Okay. Punish him and keep it moving."

"Hey, Washington? Think you can go to the cafeteria an grab me a coffee? I'm feeling kind of tired," Tahiti asked.

He looked at Tahiti like she had asked him to commit treason. "What? You fucking serious?"

"Yeah. Please?" she begged, batting her eyelashes and poking out her bottom lip.

I laughed on the inside as I watched the city-slick ex- stripper manipulate the young country guy.

"Alright. How do you want it?"

"Creamer. Two sugars. Thanks."

As soon as the door closed behind Washington, Tahiti sat on my bed and gave me one of the most delicious kisses I had ever gotten.

"Mm. Damn, girl. It feels like you missed me."

"I did. How are you doing? Do you feel better?"

"Hell yeah. Especially now that you here."

"I almost missed getting this post. Simpson called in at the last minute and took a sick day. I was supposed to be in the visiting room, but I switched with Valentine."

"That's what's up. I see you got the white boy turned out."

"Psh! Washington is a sucker, for real. He is so gullible. I'm about to have his ass running all around this hospital."

"Ha! You crazy, girl. So, what's going on back at Waupun? They trynna hang me, huh?"

"Yeah. The warden is putting you on administrative confinement when you get back. Dajuan Horn died. Marcell Carter got stabbed in the back, but you probably already knew that. They locked 37 people in the hole. Everybody is being interviewed for Horn's murder. They'll talk to you when you get back. Oh, and Big Ham is in the hole, too. I think the detectives already talked to Marcell, but he wouldn't say who stabbed him."

"Money didn't snitch on me?"

"Nope."

"I guess that don't matter 'cause they got the tape."

"No, they don't."

I looked at Tahiti to see if she was for real. "You serious? They don't got the rec tape?"

A mischievous grin spread across her face. "Nope. I accidentally deleted it."

It felt like a thousand pound weight had been lifted off of my shoulders.

"Damn, Tahiti. You a beast, ma. Come give me another kiss."

The second kiss was better than the first. It got my dick harder than steel.

"I'm not going to let anything happen to you, Luke. I got your back 100%. I know I shouldn't be telling you this, but I'm going to tell you anyway. I like you, Luke. I mean, really feeling you. I know I'm not supposed to be catching feelings, but I can't help it. I never met a man like you. When I heard you got stabbed, I was so scared and worried. I will do whatever you need me to do, Luke. For real. Don't tell Syn I told you this. She loves your ass, and I know she won't like me catching feelings for you."

"I'm not gon' say nothing. She won't like you catching feelings, but you know you just complicated everything with your revelation? We not supposed to be catching feelings, and I don't like keeping nothing from my girl."

"I know, Luke. Me either. I just wanted you to know I'm down for you, and I got your back. I wish I could find a way to get you up out of here without us having to run for our lives."

A light went on inside my head. "You got the keys?"

"No. Washington has them."

"Can you get them?"

"You want me to help you escape?"

"Hell yeah!"

"But what about your appeal? We will have to go on the run, and you don't look like you can run. Can you?"

I thought about what Tahiti said. I did have an appeal in the works, and Mike believed he could get me free. Plus, I couldn't run. Literally. "Nah, I can't run. This shit hurt too much. Plus, my lawyer saying he is going to get me out. But damn, I'ma be sick if my appeal don't work and I pass this opportunity."

"Whatever you want to do, I'll do it. But just so you know, I'll have to run with you because they gon' try to lock my ass up."

She had a point. The last thing I wanted was to be on the run with a tag-along. "Alright. Fuck it. I don't want to get you in trouble. You got your phone? I need to call Syn."

"Yeah. She doesn't know I'm working at the hospital, so she'll be super happy to hear from you."

After getting Tahiti's phone, I dialed Syn's number. "Hey, Tahiti. Have you seen or heard from Luke?" Syn answered.

"Hey, baby. I miss yo' ass so much."

There was a slight pause on her end of the line. "Luke? Oh my God, baby! Are you okay? Where are you?"

"I'm good, baby. I'm good. I'm at the hospital. Tahiti is here with me. I been here for three days. I should be going back to Waupun soon."

"Are you okay? What happened? Tahiti said you got stabbed."

"I did, but I'm good. Calico's groupies busted a move on me up at rec. I–"

The twisting of the knob on my door stopped me from talking. Tahiti jumped up and sprang into action while I slid the phone under my pillow.

"Damn, Washington. You're back fast."

"Cafeteria is only two floors away. Here's your drink. You owe me."

"How do you want me to pay you?" Tahiti flirted, taking a sip of her coffee.

"I'll think of something," Washington said, going to sit back in front of the TV.

Tahiti followed him. "What if I already thought of something?"

"Oh, yeah? What?"

"Come in the bathroom and I'll show you."

Washington looked caught off guard by Tahiti's boldness. He looked at me and then back at Tahiti. "C'mon, Johnson. You know we can't leave him alone."

"Forget Swanson. He's in cuffs. Come on in the bathroom and let me thank you. You are so hot."

Washington looked at me and then down at my cuffs. One cf my arms was cuffed to the side of the bed. "Aw, fuck it. Why not? Keep this between us, Swanson, and I'll buy you a steak from the cafeteria," Washington said as he and Tahiti walked toward the bathroom.

"Well done, Washington!" I called behind him.

Before closing the door, Tahiti mouthed to me, "Hurry up."

"Syn? You still there, baby?"

"Yeah. What happened?"

"The other C.O. came back, but Tahiti got it. She keeping him busy in the bathroom so we can talk."

"I knew it was something about that girl. We did good by getting her on the team, huh?"

I thought about Tahiti confessing her feelings for me. If Syn found out, I knew she probably wouldn't feel so good about her being on the team. "Yeah, baby. She's a beast."

"So, what happened at rec? Can they link you to the stabbing at all? Tahiti told me she deleted the recording. Do you think anybody will snitch on you?"

"I don't know, baby. Money already talked to the police, and he didn't snitch, so I don't know. You never really know with snitches."

"Do you want me to call Mike and try to get you transferred to another prison? You are getting into too much trouble in Waupun. You about to give me a heart attack from all this worry."

"Nah, I'm good. I'ma stay at Waupun. This is how it is in the joint. You gotta make a few examples before niggas respect yo' slot and let you do your time. I'm good now."

"But, Luke, I'm worried about you. I don't want anything to happen to you."

"Stop worrying, Syn. I got it. I'm more worried about this administrative confinement than them niggas."

"You gotta go to the hole?"

"Yeah. Tahiti said the warden wants me on administrative."

"That's bullshit. Can you get visits?"

"I don't know. I think all that shit is up to the warden."

"Damn, baby. I miss you so much. I want you home." Syn sounded like she wanted to cry. Hearing the emotion in her voice almost choked me up.

"I'ma be there soon. Somehow, some way. Mike said—" I stopped talking when I heard the bathroom door rattle. "Hey, baby, I gotta go. I think Tahiti is done. Give her another phone for me. I love you."

"Okay. I love you, too."

Washington came out of the bathroom first. He was sweating a little and wearing a grin that would rival Ronald McDonald's. "Everything okay, Swanson?" He asked, wiping his brow with the back of his hand.

"Yeah, man. I like my steaks well done. A potato with butter and cream on the side would be cool, too."

"Alright, I got you. Hey, Johnson, I'm going back to the cafeteria. Want anything?"

Tahiti came out of the bathroom buttoning up her shirt. "Yeah. A Sprite and a candy bar. I'll find a way to thank you for that, too," she flirted.

Washington looked like he had fallen in love. "I like the way you thank me," he cracked before leaving the room.

"Damn, Luke. That shit got me so fucking horny." Tahiti moaned as she sat on the bed and started kissing me.

I broke the kiss. "Hold on, girl! You better not be trynna kiss me after you finished sucking his dick!" I snapped.

"What the fuck, Luke? I didn't suck his dick. I wouldn't do that to you, baby. I let him suck my titties while I jacked him off."

Damn. I felt kind of stupid. "Oh. My bad. Well, in that case, do something with this," I said, freeing my hard tool from my underwear.

Tahiti leaned over and gave me some of the best head I had ever gotten. Twenty minutes later, Washington returned with my steak and potato. For the first time in a long time, I felt like a king.

J-Blunt

A Gangster's Syn 2

Chapter 21

"Well, Syn, the way I see it is you only have a couple of options. You either catch his ass at a stoplight and get on some South Central shit, or you have somebody get close to him and wait for him to slip up. Personally, I think option two is your best deal. First option is too messy. Also, you probably won't ever get close enough to him on your own to kill him. You need help, an inside man or woman," Vega explained.

We were in my office at my modeling agency. We had been going over ways to get to Calico. I wasn't a fan of the first option. There were too many what-ifs involved: innocent bystanders, police, plus I would need a small army. Option two seemed like my best move, but I didn't trust anyone enough to put them inside Calico's organization.

"Yeah. I've given it some thought, too. Option one is too messy, and two is probably my best deal, but I don't have anyone on my side I trust enough to put inside the lion's den. The last time I sent one of my girls in…" Jayda's dead stare flashed in my mind.

"Yeah. That was fucked up, what happened to Jayda. But honestly, Syn, you had to do it. Berto was a trained killer. Once he got his hands on her, it was a wrap. Just fucked up it had to be Jayda," Vega lamented.

"Yeah. I know. That's why I'm reluctant to put another one of my girls in harm's way. Plus, I can't trust too many people knowing I'm trying to kill someone, let alone Calico."

"Do you remember our chess games in prison?" Vega asked, sending me back down memory lane.

"Yeah. I remember how I used to whoop your ass," I bragged.

"Please. You know I'm the grandmaster at that shit. But the reason I brought it up wasn't to brag. I mentioned it because just like back then, I'm a move ahead of you."

I studied Vega's dark irises, trying to get a feel for what this move up on me was. "Explain."

J-Blunt

"What if I told you I manage someone from your past? Someone who you can trust, and at the same time, if you don't trust
them, said person is also expendable."

She had my full attention. "Who?"

"Now, understand this, Syn. This is a business arrangement.
This person is under contract. If you decide this person is expendable, I will have to be compensated."

"Money is not a problem. How much?"

"$25,000."

"Who is it?"

"Sophia."

I thought for a few moments. I used to fuck with a woman
named Sophia when I was in prison. No way! It couldn't be!
"Sophia from Taycheeda?"

"The one and only," Vega smiled.

"How did you find her? Where is she?"

"She's around. How I found her is not important. Like I said,
she is under contract. The next move is on you, Syn."

I took a few moments to think about Vega's proposition. I
hadn't seen Sophia in ten years. I didn't know who she had
become or what she was about. While we did have fun while we
were in prison, I never trusted her with sensitive information, and
killing Calico was very sensitive. But I did need an expendable
person.

"I'll tell you what, Vega. I like the idea of using her, but I
don't want her to know I'm trying to kill Calico, or that I even
exist. I want you to explain it to her as if you are trying to get to
him. When she finds a way to get close to him and get you in, you
call me and I'll do the rest. The fewer people who know about me
and my intentions, the better."

"Good counter move. I like the way you think, Syncere. Now,
let's talk about pay. Since I have to be more hands-on, it will cost
a little more."

"You are a Jew, Vega. How much?"

"Give me $10,000 up front. If she dies, I get $25,000 more."

"Deal."

"Damn, you're a cold-ass bitch, Syn. Remind me to never piss you off," Vega smiled, adjusting the lapels on her expensive tailored suit as she stood to leave.

"I will."

"Oh, Calico is throwing a party. I'm sending Sophia and a couple other girls. Sophia will work her magic then. Hopefully she will impress him enough to be a regular. I will keep you posted."

When Vega left my office, my mind went into overdrive. The plan we hatched had too many holes in it. Too many eyes and ears. I needed my own woman, someone to be my own set of eyes and ears and report directly to me. It made me wish Jayda was still around. I missed her so much, and the guilt from shooting her was still a constant burden. Even though I knew I had to do it, it still haunted me.

"Syncere, you have a 2:00 o'clock meeting with the photographers from *It Girl* magazine. Do you want me to reschedule?" Trinity asked as she walked in my office.

I looked down at my watch. It was 1:38. The drive to *It Girl* magazine's studio would take about 45 minutes. My meeting with Vega had gone longer than intended. "Shit. I forgot. Yeah, reschedule," I said, grabbing at my temples. I felt a serious headache coming on.

"Is everything okay?"

I looked up at Trinity and seen the concern in her eyes. She stood in the middle of my office looking like a carbon copy of me. Light brown skin, light brown eyes, and a figure most of the models I employed wished they had. She was curvy and athletic, and the tight denim jeans and halter-top showed it all. "I'm okay, Trinity. Just a little stressed."

"About what? Can I help?"

"No, I don't think so."

"Try me," she insisted.

"No. This is personal, baby girl. I have to deal with this." The last thing I wanted to do was involve her in a killing spree that had already claimed three lives.

"There you go with your secrets again. Want to know all of my business, but don't want to share yours."

"No, Trinity. It's not like that."

"Well, what is it like?" she asked, refusing to leave the matter alone.

I paused, trying to think of the words to say. If I lied to her, we would be at odds again. We were friends again, and I wanted to keep it that way. But if I told her the truth about what was on my mind, I didn't know what would happen. And I feared the unknown.

"It's complicated, okay? Really, really complicated."

"Well, good. I like puzzles," she said, walking into my office and sitting at the chair in front of my desk.

We stared at each other for a few moments. She was too damn stubborn.

"I'm not leaving until you tell me, Syncere."

We continued our stare down. I knew she wasn't leaving until I told her something.

"I'm trying to think of a way to kill Calico."

I watched her face go from astonishment to shock and then some other look I couldn't quite put my finger on. "Wow. I didn't expect to hear that."

I didn't move or say a word. I had already said too much. I should've lied.

"So, what did you come up with so far?" she asked.

Her response surprised me. "What?"

"You heard me. What do you have planned so far?"

"I don't want to talk to you about this, Trinity."

"But, Syncere, he is trying to kill you. He'll probably try to kill me too if he finds out I'm your daughter. He already had Luke stabbed. He's not going to stop until you and Luke are dead. What other choices do you have?"

It surprised me to hear my daughter speak this way. I couldn't believe she was actually condoning murder. "Do you know what you're saying?" I asked, searching her face for signs of uncertainty.

"Yeah, that Calico needs to die. What are your plans?" Her response left no doubt she was on board.

"I don't have a solid plan, yet. I'm just having a girl get close to him. Then, when he is vulnerable, they will let me know."

"You said they. Who are they?"

"Vega and one of her girls, Sophia."

"Can you trust them?"

"Vega, yes. Not sure about the other one. I'm remaining invisible to Sophia. She reports to Vega, and Vega reports to me. Everything is supposed to be getting started sometime soon. Calico is throwing a party. Sophia will be attending and will work her magic. I wish I could be there or have someone I trust go, but I don't want to put anyone else in danger."

"I'll go."

"What? Yeah, right. Are you crazy?" I said, dismissing her talk as foolishness.

"You said that you need someone you can trust. Calico has never seen me. Plus, I can watch Vega's girl. I can report right back to you."

"No, Trinity. You are not getting in this. No, no, no."

"Syncere, my life could be on the line, too. I'm tired of you running and hiding. I'm in the middle of this, too. Let me help. I can do this. Trust me."

I searched Trinity's face for the longest time. I kept thinking about what C-Money would say if he knew I put our daughter in harm's way. He would probably make a deal with the devil to allow him to come back to life long enough to shoot me. I also thought about her getting hurt. Calico was ruthless. If he found out she was my daughter, he would kill her.

But we did have a slight advantage. He didn't know I had a kid. If she could pull this off and get close to him, his ass was as good as dead.

"Okay," I caved. "I'll get you into the party, but don't you get involved in anything, you hear me? You're only there to be my eyes and ears.

"Yes, ma'am," she said sarcastically.

"This is not a game, Trinity. This is serious. You could die."

"I know. Chill. I got it. Dang," she said, looking at me with questions in her eyes. I knew she wanted to say more, so I waited. "You said you didn't want to put anyone else in danger. Who else did you put in danger?"

She was way more perceptive than I thought she was. "Jayda."

"Oh. So that's how she died. She had a good funeral."

"Which is exactly why I don't want you to go. I don't want to have to pay for or go to any more funerals."

"But I thought they said Jayda and the man got killed by the same.... Wait! You did that?"

"I didn't have a choice. He was using her as a shield. He was going to kill her anyway. Berto was a trained assassin."

"Damn, Syncere. You're fucking G.I. Jane or somebody. I'm glad you're on my side."

Chapter 22

"Mr. Swanson! How are you doing today?" Detective Billson asked as I was escorted into the small interview room.

I had come back to Waupun last night, and just like Tahiti said, I was put on administrative confinement. It was a fancy way of saying I would be in the hole until the warden decided to let me out, and now it was my turn to be questioned about Buck's murder.

"I'm doing alright, Billson. Getting tired of seeing you," I mumbled as I sat down in the chair across the table from him.

He acknowledged my comment with a nod before turning to the officer who escorted me into the room. "You can leave us, officer. I'll get your attention when I'm done with him."

When the C.O. left the room, Billson got right down to business. "Two murders, Swanson, and somehow you managed to find a way to be a suspect in both. Tell me this is just a coincidence."

"This is just a coincidence."

Billson gave me a mean stare. "This is not a game, Swanson. I read your file. You're locked up for murder, and now I'm interviewing you for two murders in two months. I don't believe in coincidences. Now, how about you give me your version of what happened at rec?"

I kept my answer short and sweet. "I got stabbed, man. It's on tape."

"Well, we don't have the tape. These incompetent high school graduates either lost the recording or they didn't record it at all. Who stabbed you?"

"I don't know."

"I heard it was the dead guy. Dajuan Horn. Was it him?"

"I don't know. I had my back turned."

"How do you get stabbed twice, once in the stomach, and not see who stabbed you?"

"I don't know."

Billson looked like he was getting frustrated by my simple responses. I liked it.

"Okay, Swanson. Here's the deal. You wanna pull my fucking chain, well, I'm going to pull yours. If you don't give me something I can work with, I'm going to have the district attorney charge you with Horn's murder. I know you were involved in both murders. I know it. And I'm going to prove it and make sure you never see the free world again."

After making his declaration, Billson wore a smug look that was supposed to intimidate me. It didn't. The only reason I sat through questioning was so I could find out what he had. Didn't seem like he had much evidence. There were too many inmates involved in the fight, and they didn't have the tape. And for the time being, it didn't seem like anyone was cooperating. As far as I was concerned, the interview was over.

"In case you don't know this, Billson, I already got life. You can't do nothing worse than that. I'm done talking. Next time you want to talk to me, I will need my lawyer, Mike Thompson, present."

***

I hated being in the hole. Since I had been in prison, I had come to know the hole very well, and I still wasn't used to it. Even though I was only one month into my indefinite hole sentence, I was feeling it. The only time I left my cell was for a shower, which I only got three times a week, or some kind of professional visit, like talking to detectives or lawyers. The warden had restricted most of my privileges. No visits for three months, and when I did get any visits back, they would be no contact visits behind glass. For one hour. I only got one ten minute phone call a week, and the warden had to personally approve whoever I called. And every time I sent out or recycled mail, the warden inspected every piece.

I rolled over onto my side, careful not to put too much pressure on my bandaged wounds, and turned the page of my newspaper. I was reading the USA Today, making my way to the money section. Keeping an eye on the stock market, taxable money fund yields, and the economy was a hobby of mine. I still controlled Syn's purse, so I tried to stay on top of everything related to money.

I was scanning the page that showed major stock changes when something caught my eye. Q Batteries, an up-and-coming long-lasting battery maker, had their stocks go through the roof. Syn owned over 2,000 shares of the company. I had bought them two years ago at $32 a share. Today those shares were trading and selling for almost $500 a pop.

"Oh, shit," I muttered, hoping the paper hadn't made a typo. I searched the page for more information and found an article beside the stock column. According to the writer, the Department of Defense had invested $500 billion into Q Batteries.

"Oh, shit," I said, louder this time. I couldn't believe my eyes. And Syn probably didn't even know it. She didn't follow the stocks. She just traded and bought what I told her to. But now that I was seeing this unbelievable news, she was definitely getting my first phone call.

"Dinner," I heard a voice call on the segregation unit's P.A. system.

I pushed the paper aside and walked over to the cell door. We to be standing in the door when the officers came by with our meals or else they wouldn't stop. And as I waited by the door for the small trap to be opened, I thought I heard a familiar voice.

"Hey, Swanson," Tahiti smiled as she used her key to open my trap.

I wanted to tell her the news about Q Batteries and have her tell Syn, but the officer trailing close behind with the cart of food trays made me keep my comments to myself. "What's up, Johnson?"

"I'm okay. How are you? Stayin' out of trouble?" she asked, grabbing my paper bag dinner from the cart. I was being fed cold meals, per the warden. Usually peanut butter and jelly or cold cut sandwiches.

"I don't even know what the word trouble means," I laughed as I grabbed the bag.

"Good. I'll be doing a round later. Enjoy your meal," she smiled before closing my trap and walking away.

I pressed my face up to the glass and watched her ass bounce and sway for as long as I could. Just the sight of her turned me on. My dick ached as I remembered how it felt to be inside her. I knew there was no way for us to get it on while I was in the hole. Cameras were everywhere, and the hole wasn't her regular post. All I had now were memories.

The one of her giving me head while in the hospital popped into my head. I needed a release. I grabbed at my pants as I tossed the bag of food onto my bed.

When the bag landed, it made a funny sound, like something heavy was inside. I abandoned my thoughts of masturbation and went to look in the bag.

"Oh, hell yeah!" I smiled as I pulled out the cell phone. I dialed Syn's number first.

"Hello?"

Hearing her voice made my heart ache. She sounded like an angel. "Hey, baby," I sang, unable to suppress my smile.

"Luke? Luke! Oh, baby, I missed you so much!" she gushed.

"I missed you, too."

"How are you? Are you okay? I see Tahiti got to you."

"Yeah. I'm good. I just seen her. They got me on this bullshit-ass AC leg. I was gon' call you when I got my phone call."

"How are things going? Did the detectives talk to you yet?"

"Yeah. A couple days ago. And it's the same one that talked to me about Silk. He thinks I killed both of them."

"Damn, baby. That is not good. How do you want to handle this?"

"Ain't really much we can do. They don't got shit without the tape. We just gotta hope these niggas keep they mouths closed. It's, like, thirty of us on lockdown. He threatened to charge me, but he can't. Nobody fingerprints was on the shank. I had a towel tied on the handle."

"Plus, they don't have the tape," Syn added.

"Yeah. You and Tahiti saved my ass with that move. That was definitely a Boss Bitch move."

"I'm not going to let anything happen to you, Luke. I need you out here with me."

"Damn, girl. I don't know what I would do without yo' ass."

"Lucky for you, you won't ever have to find out."

"Oh. Before I forget, put me on the speaker and logon to tdameritrade.com."

"Why? Did I forget to do something? I don't remember this web address."

"No, you didn't forget anything. I need to show you something," I said, trying to contain my excitement.

"Okay. I'm in. What am I looking for?"

"Look for stock information on Q Batteries."

"Um, okay. What am I looking for? You know I don't understand all of these numbers."

"Look at the price per stock. You see that?"

"Uh, yeah. $498 per share, right?"

"Yeah. Do you know what that means?"

"No. What? I own some of their stock?"

"Yep. About 2,200 shares."

"Okay, Luke. You sound pretty excited about this, but I still don't get it. Did I make a lot of money?"

"Syn. you just made your first million dollars."

J-Blunt

Chapter 23

"Hey. Where you at?"

I looked up and seen Luke staring at me. I had zoned out. I was thinking about Trinity going to Calico's party tonight, but I knew I couldn't tell him that. "I'm just thinking about how good it is to see you again. I missed you so much."

"You're a bad liar, you know that?"

If there was one thing I hated about Luke, it was that he could see through me. "I'm not lying. It's true. I am happy to see you."

"I'm not doubting that. This is our first visit in almost two months. You better be happy to see me. But that's not what I'm talking about. Something else is on your mind. What is it?" he asked, probing me with an intense stare.

"Babe, can you just trust me? I don't want to lie to you, but I also don't want to tell you why I spaced out. I can't. Not right now. I will later. But not now."

He stared at me for the longest time. I thought he was about to force my hand and make me tell him, but he didn't. "Okay. I won't bother you about it now. But promise me that you will tell me when the time is right."

I breathed a sigh of relief. "I promise I will tell you when the time is right."

"Alright. That's good enough for me. Now, come on back down to earth and kick it with your man. I missed yo' ass."

"Thank you for being so understanding, and I missed yo' ass, too. I guess Chief did good by recommending Mike Thompson to us. It seems like he really has your back."

"Yeah. Once he started filing suits on the warden and damn near everybody in the department of corrections, they got spooked and let me outta the hole. Big Ham admitted to killing Buck and stabbing Money, so it wasn't no reason for them to hold everybody in the hole. Plus, they ain't got no evidence on nobody because they ain't got the tape."

"Damn, baby. Big Ham is a real nigga. He took the wrap for everybody. Even though I don't know him, I love his ass."

"Yeah. Big Ham is true. He got five life bids, so he know they can't do nothing to him. I'ma text you his information. Put, like, $10,000 on his books. Let's make it so he won't have to worry about money for a while."

"I'll Western Union it to him as soon as you text me. If you want, we can have Tahiti thank him for us, too," I offered.

"She can't. That nigga on super lockdown."

"Oh. Damn. Well, I guess the money will have to do. So, how is everything around here? Niggas looking at you crazy now that you out the hole?"

"Nah. Most of 'em know what went down, but ain't nobody sayin' shit. Like I told you before, I think I'ma be good from here on out. I just had to put in a little bit of work to let these niggas know I'm for real. Now they know."

***

After my visit with Luke, I drove the 25 minutes to my new house in Fox Lake. I had gotten it almost two weeks ago. I liked it better than my apartment because I didn't have to worry about neighbors on the other side of my walls. My closest neighbor was about a half block away. Another plus was I was right across the street from the lake. Being so close to the water made me feel at peace.

When I got home, I pulled into the driveway behind Tahiti's Camry. I liked having her around. She was growing on me, plus I loved to eat her pussy right after Luke fucked her. It made me feel close to him. Another plus was she wasn't clingy. The only problem was with me. I was started to develop some kind of feelings for her. I could feel myself getting attached. I didn't know how to feel about it because it was unfamiliar territory. In all of my years of having sex with women, I had never caught feelings. I didn't know if the feelings were from her connecting me to Luke or something else altogether.

"Hey, Scrabble. Where is your owner at?" I asked Tahiti's Rottweiler after I let myself in the house.

After jumping up on me and giving me a few licks, he headed toward the kitchen. I followed. As I walked through the house, I noticed Tahiti had added a few more things. Mirrors in the hall and big flowers in big flowerpots seemed to be surfacing from everywhere. I had left the furnishing and decorating up to her, and for the most part she had done a good job. The only problem I had was with the coloring. Her favorite color was red, so needless to say, most of the house was decorated in red.

"Hey, boss lady," Tahiti greeted me when I walked into the kitchen. She was standing over the stove, dressed in a pair of pink booty shorts and a white wife beater.

"Hey. What you got going on in here?" I asked, walking over to investigate the sweet-smelling aromas that had been tickling my nose since I walked in the house. Tahiti could cook her ass off.

"Brown sugar-rubbed brisket and baked beans with bacon and ham hocks. How's Luke?" she asked, sticking her finger into the pot of homemade barbeque sauce. When she brought her finger to my lips, I sucked it clean. The sauce was so good that I wanted to slap somebody's momma.

"He's alright. Sad that you not at work today. Damn, Tahiti, that sauce is banging."

"I know. I learned this from Sunny Anderson. But I'll take care of Luke tomorrow. Today I have to take care of you," she said, giving me a smile and a wink.

Damn. I liked her ass.

When the food was done, Tahiti served us a meal fit for queens.

"So, what are we going to do when Luke gets out?" she asked, interrupting me savoring the taste of her brisket.

"What do you mean?"

"I mean us. You, me, and Luke. We never talked about what happens when he comes home."

I was tempted to tell Tahiti how I felt about her, but I knew if I exposed my hand too early, it could bite me in the ass later, so I played it cool.

"I don't know, Tahiti. I like you, and I think you're cool, but me and Luke haven't talked long-term concerning us. What do you want!"

"I like what we have, and I don't want anything to change. I've never been in a relationship like this before, but I like it. It's different. I get the best of both worlds."

"Good point. I like it, too. And so does Luke. I don't see anything changing between us when he comes home. I think we can try out this threesome thing. As long as you know this won't be about me and you, or you and Luke. Luke is my man, and I am in love with him. You have to know, understand, and respect that."

"I do, Syn. I don't want to come between y'all. I want to be a part of both of you."

"Okay. We'll talk more about this when Luke calls. I don't want to make a decision without him, even though I know he probably won't mind."

"Okay. Now that that's over with, where do we go from that topic?" Tahiti laughed.

"I don't know, but what I do know is you put your foot in this brisket. Damn, this is good!" I said, licking the sauce off my fingers.

"Glad you like it. I love cooking. So, how are you and Trinity? Y'all still not seeing eye-to-eye?"

At the mention of Trinity, I lost my appetite. Today was a judgment day of sorts. She was attending Calico's party tonight, and I was worried. "We're okay. She's warmed up to me a lot, but you know how flaky young girls can be. But we're good right now."

"That's good. It seemed like that was–"

Tahiti was still talking, but I had tuned her out. I was thinking about Trinity. Serious doubts were nagging me about sending her to Calico's party. I had been hating the idea since I agreed to let her go. I hated the thought of my daughter being in a hotel with Vega's girls, getting ready to enter the lion's den while I was at home having brisket.

A Gangster's Syn 2

"Hey! Are you even listening to me?" Tahiti asked, snapping her fingers at me.

"I'm sorry, girl. You mentioned Luke, and now I can't stop thinking about him. I want him home so bad. Seeing him today got to me a little bit," I lied.

"Aw. I can't wait for him to come home, too. Then we could all have fun together," she smiled raising her eyebrows.

"You crazy, girl," I laughed.

"How about we make Luke a video? He has his phone. We can send it to him."

"Yeah. I like how you think. You know just what to say." I got up from the table with a smile on my face, happy to do something to keep my mind off Trinity.

When we went to our bedroom, I busied myself setting up the camera while Tahiti gathered our sex toys. She grabbed a double-ended dildo, three different vibrators, the oil, and Luke. When everything was ready. I pressed record and got naked.

We started off kneeling on the bed, fondling each other as we kissed. When we had our fill, we gave each other sensual rubdowns with the oil. After we were horny and oily, I decided to make her cum first. I lay her on her back and grabbed the vibrating dildo with the four-inch anal dildo attached. I sucked her pearl and worked the dildos into both of her holes. It wasn't long before she was screaming my name and cumming.

"Damn, Syn. That shit was good," Tahiti breathed as she crawled onto her knees and kissed me. "Now, you lay down. It's my turn."

"Hope you like this, Luke," I said into the camera as I lay on my back.

"Oh, he gon' love this," Tahiti said as she strapped on Luke.

"No. Nope," I protested. I didn't mind her using a dildo on me, but I didn't want her simulating fucking me. That was only for the real Luke.

"Girl, stop tripping. You be fucking me with Luke all the time. Now it's my turn. Let Luke see your fuck faces," she said, stroking Luke as she walked on her knees toward me.

I closed my legs and gave her the 'girl, don't make me fuck you up' look. "Tahiti, you know how I feel about that. I said no."

"C'mon, Syn. Don't you wanna show me and Luke a good time?" she pouted, straddling my closed legs.

"I said no, Tahiti. Get–"

Her kiss shut me up. The only person I liked kissing more than her was Luke. I could feel her hands parting my thighs as her tongue slipped against mine. I didn't stop her.

Before I knew it, she was between my legs with the head of Luke inside me. She broke the kiss and turned toward the camera. "Luke, this is how we wanna get fucked when you come home, nigga."

Tahiti gave me a rough kiss as she pinned my knees to my shoulders. Then she fucked me so good I could've sworn she was Luke.

***

I was awakened by the sound of my phone vibrating on the bedside table. I figured it was Luke again, calling to talk about me and Tahiti's video. It was normal for us to talk into the wee hours of the morning whenever he had a phone.

"Hello?" I answered, not bothering to check the call screen.

"Syn, wake up! We did it."

Hearing Trinity's voice had the effect of a cold shower. I was wide awake. "What do you mean, 'we did it'? Did what?" I asked as I sat up in bed.

"It didn't go the way you wanted it to, but we did it."

"You said that already. Now, tell me what 'it' is. What happened?"

"Calico wants to take me out. On a date."

I wanted to jump through the phone and choke her. "No, no, no, no, no! That wasn't a part of the plan, Trinity. You were only supposed to be my eyes and ears. No, no, no, no.

"Syncere, listen. He knows I'm not a part of the escorts. I told him Vega hired me to watch them and I'm a college student trying to earn a little extra money. I didn't do anything. He knows I'm not that kind of girl."

"No, Trinity. This is too much. You weren't supposed to get this deep in it. It's too dangerous."

"But, Syn, this is what we need. You can cut Vega and Sophia out. We can get him ourselves."

I didn't like the way she said 'we.' "I don't like this, Trinity. This isn't sitting right with me. Where are you now?"

"I'm on my way to your house. I just left his mansion in Watertown."

J-Blunt

Chapter 24

"Luke, I have something to tell you, but I don't know how to say it," Tahiti said, giving me a strange look.

We were in the welding shop. When I got out of the hole, Jack had given me my job back. After our threesome with Tahiti, the potbellied 54-year-old white man acted like we were best friends. Not only did he give me my job back, but he watched out when me and Tahiti had sex after class.

"Okay. Shoot," I said, spraying the top of her desk with a few sprays from the bottle of disinfectant. I acted like I was cleaning, but it was all for show. My fellow inmates watched Tahiti like a hawk, so I had to be extra careful when I was around her. We didn't want anyone getting suspicious. If the wrong people found out about us, it would be trouble. Dudes hated when they couldn't get in on the action. Just like Silk.

"Well. Um."

"Before she could say her piece, she was interrupted by the phone ringing. "Wait," she told me before answering the phone. "C.O. Johnson, welding shop."

While she spoke on the phone, I searched her face. It wasn't like Tahiti to be at a loss for words. Verbally, she was one of the boldest women I had ever met.

"Luke, you have an attorney visit," she said after hanging up the phone.

"A'ight. Tell me what's on your mind before I leave."

"I'll tell you when you get back. Go see what Mike wants. It might be good news."

I wanted to stay and press her for the information, but I knew I couldn't keep Mike waiting. Like she said, it might be good news.

During the walk to the visiting room, I thought about Mike's unexpected visit. The last time he popped up unexpectedly, he came with bad news. I got a sinking feeling in the pit of my stomach as I made the trek. I didn't know if I could handle any more bad news.

"Yo. Luke!"

I looked around the prison yard to see who had called my name. I seen a guy named Mill Ticket heading in my direction. He was a muscular, light-skinned dude I worked out with at times. He was also a trustee in the hole and delivered messages between me and Big Ham.

"What's good, Mill?" I asked, slowing my pace so he could catch up to me.

"What's up, Luke? I got a word from Big Ham. He said he got that ten Gs. They shipping him to a maximum fed joint in the next couple of months. He cool with that shit because you know the feds is way better than these fucked up-ass state-ass joints. He said stay up and keep yo' nose clean."

"A'ight. Tell him to call my girl if he need anything, and to send me his address when they ship him. I got this lawyer visit, so I gotta keep it moving."

"A'ight, Luke. I'ma tell 'im what you said. Stay busta free," Mill Ticket said before we parted ways.

My thoughts shifted to Big Ham as I continued my walk to the visiting room. Whatever chances he had at going home were gone. Even though he had five life sentences and had been in prison for almost twenty years, he was still actively appealing his case. But now, after admitting to killing Buck and stabbing Money, I knew Big Ham would die in prison. I owed the big man. $10,000 was nothing compared to what he had done for me.

It was then I decided that regardless of Mike's news, good or bad, I wouldn't stop fighting for my freedom. I couldn't let Big Ham's sacrifice be in vain.

After checking in the with an officer, I was allowed to go to the conference room. As soon as Mike seen me, he shot to his feet. The smile he wore let me know he didn't have bad news.

"What's up, Mike?" I asked, extending my hand for a shake.

"We did it, Luke!" he beamed.

I immediately knew what 'it' was. "You serious?" I asked, feeling my heart rate increase to almost cardiac arrest.

"Just found out about two hours ago. Court of Appeals overturned your case!"

I felt like I had won the Super Bowl. "Yes! Yes! Yes!" I yelled, doing my best Tiger Woods fist-pumping impression. I couldn't wipe the smile from my face. I wanted to run around the room and scream hallelujah like the people did in church when they caught the Holy Ghost.

"Mike, thanks, man," I said, reaching out to hug him. I even left a few tears on the shoulder of his suit.

"I told you I wouldn't give up 'til you were out."

"So, what happens now?" I asked as we broke the embrace. I was ready to go!

"I already talked to the Attorney General, and he's not going to appeal the decision. That means we won't have to wait on another decision. In a day or so you'll be shipped back to the county jail. Basically, the conviction has been thrown out and the state has to try you again. The fist thing I'm going to do is try to get you a bail. If we can fight this with you on the streets, that will go in your favor. I know they denied you bail last time, but this time we will have a different judge. I'm going to get you out, Luke."

***

I left the visit with Mike on cloud nine. I couldn't wipe the smile off my face. I didn't want to, either. What I really wanted to do was scream from the highest point in the world. It felt like I had been given a new lease on life. I couldn't wait to use the phone and tell my mom, dad, daughter, and Syn.

"You look like you got some good news," Tahiti smiled when I walked back into the welding shop.

"My case got overturned!" I beamed.

"What? Oh my! I'm so happy, Luke! So, what happens next?"

"I go back to the county jail in a couple of days. They have to re-try me."

"Aw! I'm going to miss you so much. Work won't be the same without you," she said, looking sad.

"Why you look sad? Girl, I can get bail. I will be free," I said as thoughts of the free world filled my mind. A real bed. Real food. And Syn.

"I'm not sad. I'm happy. But I am going to miss our one-on-one sessions. I know Syn is going to want you all to herself. Can we have just one more time together? Just you and me, for old time's sake!"

When I looked down at Tahiti, I could've sworn I seen tears in her eyes, but I didn't care enough to let it bother me. My case had just been overturned, and I couldn't think of a better way to celebrate than getting some pussy. "Hell yeah. But this is not the end of us, Tahiti. Me, you, and Syn will be good together."

"Okay. I'm about to go tell Jack to cancel class. Be right back."

I threw caution to the wind and slapped Tahiti's bouncing ass as she walked toward Jack's office. When I looked back at the inmate workers and students, their jaws were agape and eyes bucked. I had done what they had been dying to do.

After giving Gus and Dave a wink, I went to prepare us a pallet in the janitor's closet. As I padded the floor with a bunch of prison greens, I could hear Jack announce that class was over. Tahiti joined me in the closet a few minutes later.

As soon as the closet door closed, I was on her ass. I kissed her as we stripped. After we were naked, I laid her on the pile of clothes and climbed between her legs.

"Wait, Luke."

"What? What's up?" I asked, searching her face. My meat was throbbing to be inside of her.

"I have to tell you something." The same look of uncertainty she had given me before my attorney visit with Mike was back in her eyes, but I didn't care. I was horny.

"Can it wait 'til we done?" I asked, ready to get down to business.

"I love you, Luke."

I wasn't expecting her to say that. "I thought we talked about this already, Tahiti. You know you're not supposed to be catching feelings."

"I know. Syn told me not to fall in love with you, and I didn't want to. It was supposed to be like a job, but now it's more than that. I'm in love with you, Luke, and I want to be with you."

Her revelation should have thrown me for a loop. The look in her eyes was serious. She wanted to be with me. She wanted to be my girlfriend. But the fact we had already discussed her staying with me and Syn, and the throbbing of my dick, made me push the seriousness of the issue to the side. "Okay. We'll find a way to work this out," I said before kissing her and grabbing my tool to stick it inside her.

"Wait, Luke. One more thing."

"What, Tahiti?" I said, getting a little irritated. I was tired of talking.

"I'm pregnant."

I heard that shit loud and clear, like someone had stood on top of Mount Saint Helen and screamed it. Her words bounced around in my mind like an echo.

"I. You pregnant?" I stuttered.

"Mm-hm," she nodded.

The room seemed to get smaller as the weight of her words sank in. I was in love with Syn, but another woman, who was in love with me, was pregnant with my seed.

Shit.

"I thought you were on birth control?"

"I am. I mean, I was. As soon as I found out I was pregnant, I stopped taking the pills."

I could feel my lust fade away. Shit just got serious. "How is this even possible? Does Syn know?"

"It's possible, Luke. Birth control isn't 100%. And I haven't told Syn. I'm scared."

"And how far along are you?"

"Six weeks."

I didn't know what to say or do. I wanted to tell her to get an abortion, but I had a problem with telling her to kill a child, no matter if it was only a fetus. But I also knew Syn wouldn't be happy when she found out Tahiti was pregnant.

"Damn, Tahiti. I don't know what to say. I never considered you getting pregnant a possibility. Shit."

"I want to be with you, Luke. I want us to raise our baby. I know Syn is your girl, but I want to be your girl, too. I like Syn, but I don't love her. But if we all have to be together to make it work, I'm cool with that. I will do whatever it takes to be with you," Tahiti said, reaching up and touching the side of my face.

"Shit. You sure do know how to ruin a moment. Fuck."

"So, what now?" Tahiti asked.

I was still on top of her, resting my weight on my elbows, my pelvis touching hers, but I was no longer aroused. Her news had killed the mood. I mean, I liked Tahiti, but I didn't love her. Even though we had already talked about doing the threesome thing, I knew this baby was going to complicate everything. "I honestly don't know, Tahiti."

"I know you probably don't feel the same way about me that I feel about you, and that's okay, Luke. I don't want to pressure you or complicate anything. But can we do one thing? Please?"

"Yeah. What is it?"

"Can we make love?"

I was thrown by her request. All these months we had just been having sex. Fucking. Getting from point A to point B. But now there were emotions involved. Feelings were on the line. Her revelations had changed the game. Things were serious now, and as I looked down at her face, I seen the look of love staring back up at me. She wanted to take things to the next level. I knew I couldn't deny her request. She had been sacrificing her livelihood and freedom for me, and now we were attached by a baby.

I felt the sting of guilt in my heart as I lowered my head to kiss her. As our tongues danced and our bodies slipped against each other in a perfect, slow rhythm, the guilt grew until I could feel it all over my body. And for the first time since we had been having sex, it felt like I was cheating on Syn.

J-Blunt

Chapter 25

"Dammit. Tahiti ! Get yo' ass out that shower and come on! We have to be at court at 10:00. It's already 8:30," I screamed, wishing she would hurry up.

"I'm drying off now. I'll be dressed in ten minutes."

"Okay. If you're not ready in ten minutes, we're leaving without you."

"You're not really going to leave her, are you, Syncere?" Trinity asked, looking amused by the situation.

"I'm not about to be late to Luke's hearing for her slow ass. She knew about the court date two days ago. If she's not out here in nine minutes and fifty seconds, we're out."

Trinity laughed like what I was saying was funny, but I wasn't joking.

"So, do you think they're going to let him out?"

"I hope so. I need my baby home. It's been two years. Two whole years! Without him, I feel incomplete. I need my other half."

Trinity gave me a funny look, like she had something more to say.

"What?"

"Uh. Um," she stuttered.

"Stop bullshitting and spit it out, Trinity."

"What about Tahiti? Is she you and Luke's girlfriend? What happens with her if they let him out today?"

"She knows her place. She is not my girl or his. She is our friend with benefits. She keeps me and Luke satisfied."

"So, you're not jealous that she's been sleeping with Luke? Aren't you worried about them falling in love?"

"No. There will only be one Boss Bitch in our house. Me. She knows her role. If she gets beside herself, we will move on without her."

"I don't know, Syn. You are a better woman than me. I'm not letting no females have sex with Myron. If he ever goes to jail, he better use his hand."

"Hunger breeds strange appetites, Trinity. And a hungry person don't care what kind of silverware they eat with. I got Luke some pussy so he won't develop an appetite for ass. Plus, I want to keep my man happy and comfortable while he's in there. When I went to prison, I didn't like girls. But, shit, I got hungry. And the only thing to eat was pussy."

"Wow, Syn! Way too much information. I don't need to hear about you eating pussy," Trinity frowned.

"Well, why are you all up in my business? Don't ask me a question if you can't handle the answer," I laughed.

"Well, now I know. I won't be asking nothing more about your relationships," she said as she grabbed her phone. "Ooh, I got a text from Calico."

Hearing his name sent a chill up my spine. "What does he want?"

"Uh, he wants to take me out."

"When?"

"It doesn't say. I'm texting him back now."

"See if he's in Milwaukee. I wonder if he knows that Luke's back in the county jail."

"Uh, I don't think he's in Milwaukee. He wants to fly me out to New York."

"No, no, no, no, no, no.

"I can't say no, Syncere. We can't make him suspicious."

"Flying to another state with our enemy is not a good idea. What if he finds out who you are? I can't get to you in New York."

"If he finds out who I am, you won't be able to get to me no matter where I am."

Trinity had a point, but I still didn't want her in another state with Calico. "I don't know, Trinity. I don't like it."

"We have to get this over with as soon as possible. The closer I get to him, the faster he will let his guard down and we can catch him slipping."

I took a moment to think about what Trinity said. She had made another good point. "Alright. But you know he's not flying you out to New York without expectations?"

Trinity looked up from texting and gave me one of the most naïve looks I had ever seen. "What do you mean?"

"He's going to want some pussy. Do you think he's going to fly you all the way out to New York and not want anything? You're pretty and all, but Calico's probably had thousands of pretty girls. He's going to fly you out there, show you a good time, and then ask for some pussy."

Trinity looked scared. Shit.

"I didn't think about that. I don't know if–"

"Okay. I'm ready," Tahiti announced as she walked into the living room.

"We'll talk more about this later," I whispered to Trinity as I grabbed my phone and purse.

***

I pulled into the parking lot of the Milwaukee County Court-house at 9:44 A.M. It took us ten minutes to get through security and into courtroom seventeen. When I walked through the polished wooden doors, the first face I seen was Mrs. Swanson, Luke's mom. Next to her was Mr. Swanson. Next to him was Latia, Luke's daughter, and next to Latia was her mother, Shay.

"Hey, Syn! Hey, Trinity!" Latia smiled and waved.

"Hi, Latia. How are you doing?" I asked as me and my girls walked over to greet Luke's family.

"Good. Can't wait to see my daddy. I hope they let him out today."

"Me, too, baby girl. Hi, Mr. and Mrs. Swanson."

Mr. Swanson gave me a weak, "Hey." Mrs. Swanson gave me a grunt and rolled her eyes, and Shay gave me a stank look. I wanted to reach my arm back and slap all three of them with one motion like they did on the Three Stooges show, but I didn't. I bit my tongue and kept it moving.

187

"Damn, Syn. What was all that about?" Tahiti asked after we had seats in a pew two rows over from Luke's people.

"It's a long story, Tahiti. One that I don't feel like telling right now."

"They haters, Tahiti," Trinity spoke up. "They think he locked up because of Syn, so they be giving us shade."

"Oh. Damn. That's messed up. Who's the dark-skinned girl that was looking like she wanted to get her ass stomped?" Tahiti asked, shooting a nasty look at Shay.

"That's Luke's stankin'-ass, no good-ass, thot-ass baby momma," I spat.

"Really? She looks–"

Tahiti paused when a side door to the courtroom opened and in walked Mike Thompson and the man of the hour. When I seen Luke, my heart skipped a beat, pulse quickened, and pussy jumped. Luke was wearing an orange jumpsuit and shower thongs, but even in the jail getup, my man looked good.

After smiling and waving at us and his family, he sat next to Mike at the conference table in front of the judge's bench. At the table next to Luke and Mike was District Attorney Mitchell Sellers.

I was staring at the back of Luke's head when the door to the judge's chamber opened. Out walked an old white woman with brown hair. She was also wearing a judge's robe. Her name was Jessica Charles. According to Mike, she was one of the fairest judges in the courthouse.

"Alright. What do we have before us?" the judge asked her clerk.

"Case number 14CF120. State of Wisconsin versus Luke Swanson. Set today for a bail hearing. Appearances, please?"

District Attorney Sellers shot to his feet. "State appears by District Attorney Mitchell Sellers."

Mike stood next. "The defense appears in person and by attorney Mike Thompson."

"Alright. This is a requested bail hearing by the defense. I have read over the case and will allow both parties to present their arguments before I rule. Mr. Sellers, the floor is yours," the judge said before reclining in her chair.

"Your Honor, the state is requesting you deny bail for Mr. Swanson. This is based on the seriousness of the offense, the need to protect the public, and the need to protect Mr. Swanson. This case involves several wild western-type shootouts with at least three attempts being made on the defendant's life. Mr. Swanson has some sort of beef with real life gangsters who don't mind shooting up businesses and entire neighborhoods. We ask that the defendant remain in custody to protect any innocent bystanders if another attempt is made on his life. We must protect the community from Mr. Swanson and his bedfellows. That is all."

I wanted to jump up and slap Mitchell Sellers' punk ass. Re always twisted shit. And from the look on the judge's face, it looked like she was buying the bullshit he was selling."

"Okay, Mr. Sellers. Mr. Thompson, your turn."

Mike smoothed the wrinkles from his navy suit as he stood. I hoped that gesture meant he was about to give a good speech.

"Your Honor, the defense asks that you honor Mr. Swanson's constitutional right and set him a bail. As you know, this is not a case about gang members, drugs, or any kind of street beef. Mr. Swanson is a college graduate, a respected colleague at one of the most prestigious accounting firms in the nation, and an overall upstanding citizen who pays his taxes and votes. Mr. Swanson has no gang affiliations and was dragged into this unfortunate situation because of his unwillingness to participate in criminal activity. This is a self-defense case, your honor. Mr. Swanson was protecting his life when he fired his weapon. He was shot. In front of his residence. Mr. Swanson is not a threat to the community. He wants to go home to be with his loving parents, his daughter, and girlfriend. He has been punished long enough, your honor. Since when did we start punishing people for protecting themselves? We again ask that you grant bail."

I couldn't wipe the smile from my face. Mike had done a good job. I could already feel Luke's hands all over my naked body.

"I've listened to both parties, and you've both made good points. Unfortunately the risk to the public is too great. It appears that whoever is hunting you, Mr. Swanson, doesn't care much about who is present when they go after you. I cannot put the public at such a risk. So, for the sake of public safety, I will deny your request for bail at this time. Your defense team must come up with a plan to keep the public safe before I set bail. I will reconsider this matter in one week."

Punk-ass bitch!

Chapter 26

She could feel the butterflies flying around in her stomach as she disembarked the plane. What she was doing was beyond risky. If things went sour, death was certain. But if things went right, peace for her and her loved ones would be on the horizon. And for that reason she allowed her feet to lead her off the plane and into the airport.

LaGuardia Airport made people seem famous, even if they weren't. The camera flashes from the paparazzi, the looks people who knew you weren't from New York gave you, and the hypnotizing effect the city had on people who had seen the city for the first time all made a layman feel special.

"Miss Baily?" called a black man in a dark tux.

She looked up and spotted the cleanly-dressed man standing in a crowd of people who had been waiting for loved ones to get off the plane. After giving him a big smile and a half-wave, she headed in his direction, her carryon suitcase rolling behind her.

"Mr. Majors?" she asked after closing the distance.

"Yes, ma'am. Allow me to get that," the well-spoken and neatly-dressed man said as he reached for her bag.

"Certainly. It's nice to meet you, Mr. Majors. New York is a beautiful city."

"The pleasure is all mine, Miss Baily. And New York is more than just a beautiful city. It is the heartbeat of America. A concrete jungle where dreams are made," he smiled.

After their introduction, Mr. Majors escorted her from the airport to a waiting limo. During the ride to her hotel, she tried to focus on the sights and sounds of the city and not on the millions of thoughts that roamed around in her mind. She couldn't believe she was actually in New York. And not only that, she would be going on her third date with an enemy of her family.

While she rode in the limo, hiding behind her false identity, she allowed herself to have thoughts about the man she was supposed to beguile. He was her kind of man. Not only was he good looking and rich, but he was powerful. He exuded power when he walked, talked, and gestured. The people around him moved quickly when he gave a command, and whenever they were in public and ran into someone who knew him, they looked at him with awe and respect. Like they were in the presence of Hollywood royalty.

"Today you will be staying at the Trump Tower, ma'am. Your things will be brought up to your room," Mr. Majors called from the front seat as he pulled the limo to the curb.

Heather looked out the window and up at one of the tallest buildings she had ever seen. Her face was still pressed up against the window when the door opened.

"Oh. Sorry, ma'am," a neatly-dressed bellhop apologized when he saw Heather almost fell from the car.

"It's okay. It was my fault. This building is huge," she smiled, allowing the man to help her from the car.

"Trump Tower is one of the finest buildings in all of America. Mr. Calico is waiting for you upon the roof," the man said as he led her across the expensive red carpet and into the luxurious building.

Heather took it all in as she followed her escort. Shiny marble floors, gold accents, a crystal chandelier, and even a few B-list celebrities filled the lobby.

When they got to the elevator bay, the man eyed her as he pressed the call button. "My goodness, you are stunning. Are you on TV? Been in any movies?" he asked, looking her over.

Heather was beautiful, but not in an overly glammed way. Her skin was the color of fine sand, her face was small and round, and her thick eyebrows were perfectly arched over her slightly slanted, light brown eyes. She had a small nose, a small top lip, but her bottom lip was full and ripe. She purposely wore her makeup light – just a little blush on her cheeks, some eye shadow to make her eyes pop, and lip-gloss. Her hair had been curled with giant rollers, and as a result, her hair hung in big, loose curls that flowed just past her shoulders. Her clothing choice was a simply-knit white maxi dress that showed off her athletic build.

"Thank you, sir. No movies or TV. Just some print stuff," she blushed.

"Mr. Calico is truly a lucky man," the man smiled.

"Thank you."

When the elevator opened, her escort left her as she stepped in. Inside the elevator was another man dressed in an identical suit as the bellhop. "What floor?" he asked.

"Uh. The roof, I think," she fumbled.

"Oh. A guest of Mr. Calico? Yes?" he asked, pressing a button on the gold display panel.

"Yes."

The elevator ride was smooth, and operatic music played in the background. When the car finally got to the roof, the door chimed as it opened. What Heather saw took her breath away. "Oh my!"

Seeing the helicopter idling on the rooftop heli-pad had her speechless. Calico and two of his bodyguards were standing a few feet from the chopper. When she stepped onto the roof, he strode confidently toward her, wearing his trademark tailored white suit.

"My, my, my. This should be a crime," he smiled, flashing his cinematic smile. Calico took good care of himself. At 41, his light complexion didn't have a wrinkle or blemish. The spa treatments and facials kept his skin looking youthful, and since he valued his appearance, a manicure and pedicure was also a must.

As Heather took him in, she noticed his normally ponytailed hair was hanging loose and blowing in the wind. It made her think of The Rock in the movie *Hercules*.

"What are you talking about?" she asked, looking back and forth from him to the helicopter.

"Looking this good. It should be a crime," he smiled, giving her a kiss on the cheek.

"Aw, thank you. What is this?" she asked, looking at the flying machine.

"I have a few connections in this city. My brother and The Donald are aces. He loaned me his helicopter. I wanted to show you the city from a bird's eye view. I love New York. Looking at the city from the sky is exciting."

During their flight over the Big Apple, Heather had a hard time seeing Calico as the bad guy. He treated her like a queen. How she imagined a man would treat a woman.

After their flight, Calico treated her to dinner at a five-star restaurant. From there they went to a private party hosted by P. Diddy. There were so many stars in the place that Heather felt like she was in a movie, and the attention they showed her and Calico was unforgettable.

"Did you enjoy the evening?" Calico asked as they rode through the illuminated city in the back of a limo. They were sitting side-by-side, his arm draped around her shoulders.

"Oh, my God! I don't ever remember having so much fun in my life. Helicopter rides, eating North Atlantic Swordfish in a five-star restaurant, and a party with Puffy. I can't believe I actually met Usher," Heather gushed.

"Yeah. He's cool. So, how did you get hooked up with Vega? A woman of your caliber doesn't seem like she hangs out with lesbian pimps."

"I don't. Well, not really. She's a friend of the family. My mom's friend, actually. She knows I like the fashion industry and asked me if I wanted to attend a party. Be her eyes and ears. I needed the money, so I agreed."

"Well, there are certainly better ways to get money and get into the fashion industry than keeping an eye on whores. Is that what you're going to school for? Fashion?"

"Yes."

"Where did you say you attend?"

"Alverno. I do most of my classes online, but every now and then I have to go to class."

"So, your schedule is flexible?"

"Yes."

"Good. I like flexible," he flirted, trailing a hand along her thigh.

Heather was intoxicated by Calico. The way he looked at her sent shivers through her body. He wanted her, and surprisingly, she wanted him. So much so that when he leaned his face toward hers, she met him halfway. She closed her eyes and got lost in the moment. Although she was kissing him for the first time, to her it felt like she had been kissing him her whole life.

"Stay with me tonight," Calico said, breathing heavily.

Heather felt like she was flying amongst the clouds. To have one of the most powerful men she had ever met desiring her so badly was better than any sensual stimulant or aphrodisiac she had ever heard of. The element of danger that was involved only heightened what she was feeling.

"Okay," she agreed, leaning forward to kiss him again.

When they got to his suite at Trump Tower, Calico led her to his master bedroom. There was a canopy bed inside with soft-looking white curtains hanging around it. The sheets on the bed were 5,000 count Egyptian.

After parting the curtains, Calico sat on the bed and pulled her between his legs. "I have been waiting on this moment for weeks," he said before kissing her.

Heather received his touch welcomingly. Calico lit fires inside her that she had never known. A fire her boyfriend Myron never knew existed.

"Let me take this off," he said, tugging at her dress.

Heather lifted her arms and allowed him to pull the garment over her head. After throwing the dress aside, Calico eyed her body like he was a hungry lion and she was prey. Heather's body looked flawless in the white Victoria's Secret bra and panty set. He leaned forward and placed a kiss on her flat stomach as he reached behind her to undo her bra. When he pulled it off, the nipples on her 34C's pointed at him like little fingers.

"Mm!" she moaned, cradling Calico's head as he sucked her breasts.

"Come lie down," he said, helping her onto the bed. When she was lying comfortably on her back, Calico stood to undress. She watched through the sheer curtain as he stripped. Calico's body was toned like he had a gym membership, and he topped it off with a nice-sized package.

"Relax, Heather. Let me show you how it will be when you are with me," he said smoothly as he climbed onto the bed.

Syn's words echoed in her mind as he pulled off her panties. *Do not get attached to him. Do not get attached to him. Your pussy is a tool. This is a job. Stay focused on the mission.*

When Calico's tongue flicked across her clit, Syn's words exploded into a million pieces and blew to the back of her mind. The danger and fear, combined with her lust, swirled around inside of her like a tornado.

When she came, it was epic. The best orgasm she had ever had.

When he mounted and penetrated her, she knew she had gotten herself in a world of trouble.

Chapter 27

One Week Later

I was going out of my mind with anxiousness. I wanted to stand up, but when I stood up, I wanted to sit back down. When I sat back down, I wanted to stand again.

Scrabble looked at me like something was wrong with me. "I'm okay, boy. Just a small case of the jitters," I lied to the dog.

I wasn't okay, and I didn't have a small case of the jitters. I had a huge case of the jitters. The reason? Luke was free. Well, sort of. He was out on bail. He and Mike Thompson would be pulling up to the house at any minute. I was an excited and nervous wreck.

The fight for Luke's semi-freedom wasn't easy. It took two weeks of constant bail hearing battles with Mitchell Sellers and $100,000 to set him free. It was the best money I ever spent. Truthfully, I would have given every dime I had to get Luke back on the streets. And I would've been in the car with him and Mike, except I had to be at home to let the D.A.'s people and the phone company come and hook up Luke's electronic monitoring system.

As a condition of Luke's release, he had to be on the bracelet while Mitchell Sellers re-built his case against him. I didn't care about any of that. I just wanted him home.

When Scrabble began barking at the door, I tore out of the house like I was a member of the U.S. track team. I could hear Scrabble barking behind me, giving chase as I ran toward Mike's green BMW that had pulled into my driveway.

By the time Luke got out of the passenger seat, I was already airborne, leaping into his arms. "Luke! I'm so happy you're home, baby!" I cried as I slobbered all over him.

"Hey, Superwoman," he groaned as we hugged and kissed.

"If my wife greeted me like that every time I came home, I probably wouldn't ever leave," Mike cracked.

I ignored Mike, wrapping my legs around Luke's waist and kissing him some more.

"Get a room."

Hearing the woman's voice gave me an instant buzz kill. I looked over Luke's shoulder and seen his mother, father, and daughter getting out of a tan Chevy Avalanche. I sobered up at the sight of his parents. "Hey, Mr. and Mrs. Swanson. Hey, Latia," I grumbled as I climbed off of Luke.

"Hello, Syncere," his mother said, giving me a look of disdain. I knew we were going to have a confrontation. Soon.

"Hey, Syncere," his father said, saying my name like it left a bad taste in his mouth.

I wanted to say, "Fuck you, too," but I didn't. Latia was running toward me, and I wanted to be all smiles for her.

"Hi, Syncere!" Latia beamed, giving me a big hug.

"Hey, baby girl! You are getting so big and cute."

"Well, my job here is done," Mike spoke up. "Call me if you need anything, Luke. I'll keep you informed of all the court dates."

"Will do. Thanks again, man," Luke said as they shook hands.

When Mike left, I invited the family into the house. "Did somebody die in here?" Luke asked as soon as we walked in.

"Tahiti likes red. I left the decorating up to her."

"I like it," Latia said.

"Reminds me of blood. Or tomatoes," Mr. Swanson said.

"I think you need to put whoever decorated this in prison," Mrs. Swanson said, looking around the living room like it was painted in actual blood.

I wanted to tell her ass to get out if she didn't like it, but I didn't. I just rolled my eyes.

"Funny you should say that, Mom, 'cause the girl who did the decorating works in a prison," Luke laughed.

"Can I get anyone drinks? Something to eat?" I asked, trying to be a good host.

Mr. and Mrs. Swanson declined. Latia and Luke wanted drinks. I went and got flavored waters. When I came back into the living room, everyone was seated and talking. I snuggled up next to Luke and wrapped my limbs around him.

"Hey, where's Trinity? Why is she not at my homecoming?" Luke asked, looking around like she was about to jump out and surprise him.

"Um, she had to take care of something back in L.A. She should be here later tonight or tomorrow morning."

Luke gave me a look that let me know he knew I was lying. I hated that shit.

"So, what happens now, son?" Mr. Swanson asked.

"Another trial, I guess. For some reason the D.A. wants me in jail."

"What are your chances of beating it this time? Have to be good since they overturned your case on appeal."

"I don't know, Pop. Hard to say. I thought I would get self-defense the first time. But I trust Mike. Hell, he got me out from under a life sentence."

"No, Mike didn't do it. Jesus did it," Mrs. Swanson corrected.

"I don't care who did it. Mike, Jesus, or Buddha, I'm just happy to be free," Luke laughed. I couldn't have agreed with him more.

It took forever for his parents and Latia to leave. At one point during the evening I considered getting bitchy and kicking everybody out, but I knew that wouldn't help my standing with his parents, so I sucked it up and waited. Then, when I was right on the verge of running out of patience, his father decided it was time for them to go. They had been at our house for almost six hours, five hours too long.

As soon as they left, I was on Luke's ass like a bear on a honeycomb. We were still in the living room, on the couch. He was sitting down, and I was straddling him, trying to suck his lips off his face. I stopped kissing him long enough to pull his shirt off.

"Where's Tahiti? She's off work, ain't she?" he asked.

"Told her not to come home tonight. This is our night. Why? I'm not enough?"

"It's been a couple of years, baby. Don't know if you can handle all this pent-up lust by yourself," he laughed.

I thought I seen something more in his eyes, but I ignored it. I wanted him in the worst way. "I can handle your ass. But don't worry, she'll be around. Tonight is our night. We'll let her in tomorrow. And just so you know, it's only enough room for one Boss Bitch. She is not *your* girl. She is *our* girl."

"Wouldn't have it any other way," he smiled.

When me and Luke were finally naked, I laid him back on the couch and just looked at him. The naked pictures I had of him were nothing like the real thing. He was the total package: good looking, a great body, and a spell-casting magic stick. "Wait here," I told him as I got up and went to the kitchen.

"Ooh! I read about that shit," Luke smiled when he seen the ice tray. Inside the tray were flavored ice cubes.

"Let's make it real," I said as I sat the tray on the table and knelt beside Luke. I took a cherry-flavored cube and dragged it across his chest. He shuddered, and his nipples got hard. I ran the cube across his nipples and sucked them. From there I trailed the cube across his abs and sucked up the pooling liquid trail. When that cube melted, I grabbed another one and ran it along the length of the real Luke.

"Shh! Shit!" he hissed, arching his back.

That shit got me excited. I took him in my mouth while I ran the ice cube all over his balls.

"Shh! Ah, damn! Mm!" he moaned, sounding like he was caught between pleasure and pain. I loved it! And for my finale, I popped a cube in my mouth and gave him the hot-and-cold dick sucking of his life. When he came, it was thick and gooey. I drank it all like it was a Slurpee.

"Shit, girl!" he panted, sucking in deep gulps of air.

"Told you I can handle it. Question is, can you handle me?" I asked, stroking his meat. He was still hard.

"Why don't you climb aboard so we can find out?"

I was dying to get him inside of me. I moaned as I sat down on top of him, relishing how good he felt inside of me. He fit me perfectly. Tahiti and the fake Luke were a good substitute, but there was nothing like the real thing. And after I got used to him

200

being back inside of me, I rode his pole like I was one of the strippers I employed.

He came once, I came twice. After my second orgasm, he took control. He gave it to me from behind just how I liked it. I screamed so much that I lost my voice.

***

"I missed you so much, Luke," I cooed as I lay on top of him. We were still on the couch. My head was resting on his chest. I was running my fingers over his bullet wounds.

"Shit. That's an understatement, baby. I was in there feeling like J-Holiday. *I can't breathe when you talk to me. I suffocate when you're away from me,*" he sang, tearing up one of my favorite songs.

"Stop! J-Holiday is going to sue your ass," I laughed.

Being with Luke felt right, just like old times. I felt safe and complete. Whole. I never wanted to be without him again.

"I'm scared, Luke," I confessed, feeling the tears well up in my eyes.

"Of what, baby? I'm here now."

I sat up to stare at him. "I'm scared to lose you again. Those were the hardest and loneliest two years of my life. I don't ever want to go through that again."

"And hopefully you won't. We have to trust in Mike, babe. Hopefully he can pull another rabbit out of his hat."

That wasn't good enough for me. "Let's run away, Luke. Let's leave the country. I still have over $800,000 in cash and assets. We could survive anywhere."

"Nah, baby. I can't. I have to fight this. I don't want to be on the run for the rest of my life. We gotta put this behind us. I want my life back."

"Yeah, you're right. I guess I'm just a little paranoid. I don't want to lose you again," I was saying when my phone rang.

"Same here. Who is that?"

I checked the screen. "Daughter."

"Tell her I said she better be here by the morning or it's on," he threatened.

"Will do. Hey, baby girl."

"Mom, I need help."

The first thing I noticed was she called me mom. It was the first time ever. The second thing I noticed was the tone of her voice. She sounded terrified.

"Where are you? Are you okay?" I asked, feeling the panic rise up inside of me.

"He knows who I am. I'm in the trunk of a car. They didn't find my phone," she whispered.

"What's wrong?" Luke asked.

I ignored him. "Where are you now?"

"I don't know. I think we're still in Milwaukee. I. Wait. The car is stopping. I have to go. Help, Mom!"

"Trinity? Trinity!" I screamed into the phone as the line went dead.

"Syn, what's wrong? What happened to Trinity?" Luke asked.

I felt numb inside, like my world was crashing down. I didn't know what to do or say. It felt like I was in shock.

"Syn, where is Trinity? What happened?"

Luke's voice brought me back from the abyss I had fallen into. "Calico's got her." The words came out like a whimper, but Luke heard me.

"What? How the fuck did he find her? I thought she was in L.A.?"

I wanted to answer him, but I couldn't. Not only did I have trouble putting my words together, I also didn't want him to know I was keeping secrets.

"Syn, you gotta talk to me, baby. What the fuck is going on? Why aren't you talking? Where is Trinity? How did Calico get Trinity?"

I looked over at Luke and seen anger, worry, and fear swirling around in his eyes. Then something inside of me clicked. I had to go get my baby!

"I can't explain it right now, Luke, but I have to go. I have to find her," I said, snapping into action and running toward my bedroom.

Luke was on my heels. "Syn, what the fuck is going on?" he yelled, grabbing my arm and spinning me around. There was a determined look in his eyes. A look that let me know I wasn't leaving the house without answering his questions.

"Do you remember when we were on a visit a little while back, when you got off of administrative confinement, and I was spacing out and wouldn't tell you why?"

He thought for a moment and then nodded.

"Well, I came up with plan to get Calico."

"No, Syn! Why? Why didn't you wait? You know the Trigga Klan was going to do it."

"They wasn't moving fast enough. What was I supposed to do, just sit around like everything is cool? Like he wasn't out looking for me? You know he isn't going to stop looking for me. He wants his money and my life."

Luke just stared at me. He knew I was right. "Damn, Syn. I wish you would've told me about this. How did Trinity get in this? He didn't know you had a daughter, did he?"

"No. She wanted to help me get to him. I didn't want her to do it, but she kept insisting. She was supposed to get close to him and let me know when he was vulnerable. So I could kill him."

"Shit, Syn. You shouldn't have let her go. Where are they?" he asked, going into the room and grabbing some clothes out of the drawer.

I followed him and grabbed the pants he was about to put on. "I don't know where they are, but you can't leave."

He snatched the pants away from me and put them on. "Fuck if I ain't."

"No, Luke. I will handle this. I have to finish this. You already sacrificed enough. If you leave, they will lock you up. Let me do this."

"I can't sit this one out, Syn. I can't let nothing happen to you or her," he said as he threw on a dark t-shirt.

I stood in front of him. "I can't let you do this, Luke. Let me finish what I started. I already have blood on my hands."

"Who's blood? What are you talking about?"

"I had to kill a couple of people to get to Calico. Rhoda, Jayda, and Berto."

Luke's eyes looked like they were about to pop out of his head. "You killed Jayda?"

"I had to do it. Berto was going to kill her."

"Who the fuck is Berto?"

"The Hawaiian you beat up. I used Jayda to get to him, but he grabbed her and was going to kill her. He was using her as a shield. I didn't have a choice."

He shook his head from side to side, looking as if it was hard to believe what I was saying. "And Rhoda? Who was that?"

"She use to be my friend until she testified against me. She was part of the reason I went to prison. She was Rasheed's girlfriend. She started all this. She was the one who told Calico I was out of prison."

Luke became silent, just staring at me, his mouth open slightly. The look was of awe and wonder, like he couldn't believe what I was telling him. I took advantage of his silence and grabbed his face to look him in his eyes.

"Please, Luke. Stay here. Let me finish this. Don't go back to jail for me. I need you home. I can do this. Trust me."

A dejected looked flashed across his face. I knew he wanted to protect me. He had gone to prison for me. He loved me and would give his life for me, but I didn't want him trading his life for mine. I wanted to protect him. He had already sacrificed enough. I had changed him. Made him a killer. Got him involved. I didn't want to involve him any more.

"Syn, I swear to God, your ass better be careful," he said, letting a single tear fall from his eye.

Seeing him cry touched me. It wasn't a weak gesture. I seen love, true love. I had to come back to him. "I promise I'll be careful. I don't know where she is, but I will find her."

"She got GPS on her phone. As long as he phone is on, you can track her. What's that?" Luke asked, eyeing the black case I had pulled from under the bed.

"My treasure chest." I opened the case and revealed the contents. Inside were guns and ammo. Two Glock-17s with silencers, an AR-15, and a .357 revolver.

Luke looked at the gun cache like it was a pot of gold. "When did you get all this shit?"

"When you were away. Had to be able to protect the house if Calico came looking for me."

J-Blunt

Chapter 28

I left the house with the two Glock-17s on my lap, speeding toward Milwaukee. Trinity's GPS was working. I was able to keep track of her on my phone. She had stopped moving somewhere in downtown Milwaukee. I prayed for my baby girl as I rolled down the highway, hating myself for allowing her to get involved. I knew better. If Calico hurt my daughter, I would never be able to forgive myself.

It took thirty minutes to get to the GPS coordinates. It was an old shipping yard. I looked around and seen lots of condemned warehouses. After parking by a rusted-out gate, I got out of the car to look around. It was dark outside and the shipping yard was barely lit. All I had was the moonlight to guide me. I tucked a Glock in my pants and kept the other one in my hand as I looked around for the warehouse Trinity was in. It didn't take long to find her. It was the only warehouse with lights on.

I crept up to the building and looked through a dusty window for signs of life. I spotted Trinity. She was tied to a chair. Something was tied around her mouth, but otherwise she looked unharmed. I continued to look around the warehouse for Calico. I didn't see him or anyone else. The entire scene seemed set up. It was too easy. Did they really bring her here and leave her? I didn't think so. Something was up.

I left the window and began a search of the rest of the building. I needed to find a way to get in without being seen or heard. It took a couple of minutes, but I found a back door. It was being blocked by a big and old-looking tire. I sat my gun down to try to move it. It was heavy as hell, but knowing my daughter was inside gave me the strength of ten women.

I was able to move the tire a couple of feet when I heard a noise behind me. I turned my head just in time to see someone racing toward me.

It was Berto! How the fuck could it be Berto?

I let go of the tire and went for the gun on my waist. I gripped the handle and drew the weapon. Before I could point it at him,

Berto jumped in the air and dropkicked me in the chest. I soared through the air like I was weightless and slammed into the side of the building. I looked to my left and seen my other gun. I tried to grab it, but Berto was upon me before I could reach it. He punched me in the face so hard I blacked out.

The first thing I noticed when I came to was the smell. Calico had his own scent. It smelled like a bunch of colognes mixed together. I didn't even have to open my eyes to know he was near.

Upon opening my eyes, Calico came into view. He stood about ten feet away from me. He was dressed in an all-white suit and smiling like he was happy to see me. He had two men with him: Berto and a man who looked like he ate the weights after he lifted them. He could have been a real life Incredible Hulk.

"Oh, shit! Look who's awake, y'all. Pam Grier is back," Calico cracked.

His henchmen laughed like Calico was Steve Harvey. I looked around and seen I was tied to a chair. Trinity was in a chair next to me.

"Let her go, Calico. You got me. I'll give you the money."

"Y'all hear this shit? She want me to let the bitch go that was gon' serve me to her on a platter," he laughed. "But you know what, Loretta? I'ma take your advice. Get up, Trinity."

I thought my ears was playing tricks on me. He called her Trinity? What did he know? How did he know?

When I looked over and seen my daughter shake off the ropes that were around her wrists and stand up, I got my answer.

"That's right, baby. Come here," Calico said, holding a hand out to her. I felt sick to my stomach. I wanted to vomit. My head hurt. I felt like it was about to explode. And my heart? It was crushed. I wanted to scream as I watched Calico wrap an arm around Trinity's shoulder and pull her close.

"Don't look so surprised, Loretta. Or should I say, Syn? Yeah. Syn fits you to a tee You's a deadly bitch. Killed my nigga Berto, your own girl, and Rhoda's fat ass. Trinity told me everything. How you wasn't there for her. How you lied about being her

208

cousin. That C-Money is her daddy. Oh, and by the way, this is Veto, Berto's brother. He wanted to kill your ass, but I couldn't let him do that. This shit is too personal. What I'm going to do is let the woman you birthed, who exchanged her life for yours, take you out. How that sound?"

I couldn't talk. I was so mad and hurt that I started to cry. My daughter betrayed me. I knew pleading with him would get me nowhere, so I didn't even bother. All I could do was cry silently and drown in my regrets. I shouldn't have let Trinity get involved, and I should've brought Luke.

"Don't cry, Syn. You had a good plan. Almost worked. But the thing about me is I'm a boss. I have my people check everybody I come in contact with. Did you know that Heather Bailey doesn't attend Alverno College? And I'll do you one better. Heather Bailey of Wisconsin lives in Portage. And she's white. When I figured out the name was fake, I knew you was behind this. You killed Berto and Rhoda, and now you was coming for me. Lucky for me, Trinity and Vega don't understand the concept of loyalty. Fear of death is a great motivator. Alright, enough of the bullshit. Kill your mother, girl."

Calico pulled a black automatic handgun from his waist. After taking out the clip, he held the gun out for Trinity. She kept her head down, tears streaming down her face, refusing to take the gun or look up at me. Even though she betrayed me, seeing her tears tugged at my heart. She was sorry, And I was, too. Because if I made it out of this alive, I was going to kill her.

"C'mon, now, Trinity. Either you kill her or I kill you. We already talked about this. You have one shot. Put it in her head and get it over with," Calico urged.

Trinity took the gun and walked toward me with her head down. Damn. This was really it. My daughter was about to kill me. I couldn't go out like this. "He is still going to kill you," I whispered.

Trinity paused to look at me. I seen fear, uncertainty, and guilt swirling in her eyes. She didn't know what to do, but she also didn't want to die.

"Give me a gun, Veto," Calico ordered. The goon handed him a pistol, and Calico pointed it at Trinity. "I don't got time for this shit. Kill her or I'm killing you."

"I'm sorry, Mom," Trinity cried, lifting the gun to my face. Her arm shook like she had Parkinson's Disease. I watched her finger apply pressure to the trigger.

Then she spun and pointed the gun at Calico. Their guns fired at the same time. Trinity's bullet missed. Calico's hit her in the chest. She screamed and fell to the ground.

"Stupid-ass bitch!" he cursed, walking to stand over my daughter. "I gave you life and this is how your back stabbing-ass does me? I got something for you. Veto, give me that knife and take this gun."

Veto pulled a long, shiny knife from his belt and gave it to his boss. It looked like the one Sylvester Stallone had in the movie *Rambo*. Trinity squirmed on the ground, crying and gasping for air, holding her chest wound. The fear of death gripped her as Calico stood over her with the knife.

"Calico, I swear to God, if you touch her–"

Before I could finish my threat, he cocked an arm back and slapped me so hard that a white light went off in my head. "Shut the fuck up, bitch! Don't threaten me. You–"

Pop-pop-pop-pop-pop-pop-pop-pop-pop-pop-pop-pop-pop-pop!

Gunfire rang out, scaring the shit out of me. Veto and the black Incredible Hulk let out death moans as they fell to the ground. Their bodies twitched as blood pooled around them.

Calico reacted quick, grabbing me out of the chair and using me as a shield.

"Let her go, Calico!"

"I couldn't believe it was him! "Luke!" I called, searching the darkness for my man.

"Show yourself, nigga, or I'ma kill this bitch," Calico yelled, pressing the knife to my throat.

Luke appeared from the shadows, pointing the AR-15 at us. "Let her go, Calico!"

210

"Shoot his ass, Luke! Shoot him!" I screamed. I knew he couldn't shoot Calico without shooting me, but I didn't care. I wanted him dead so bad that I didn't mind dying with him.

"Go ahead, Luke. Shoot," Calico taunted. "See if your bitch is bulletproof."

Luke kept the gun pointed at us, moving slowly, trying to get an angle. "Let her go, Calico. Let's do this man-to-man."

"Fuck that, nigga. Put the gun down or I'ma kill her," Calico ordered. I could feel blood trickle down my neck as the blade cut my skin.

"I can't put it down. You got a hit out on us."

"You got three seconds or I'm killing her. One."

"Shoot us, Luke! Please. Do it," I begged.

"Two."

"Do it! Shoot us!"

"Three."

"Ah!" I screamed as the knife went through my thigh.

"Put the gun down or the next stab is doing in her heart."

"No, baby. Don't do it. Shoot him!" I yelled, ignoring the pain shooting up and down my leg.

"I gotta do it, baby," Luke said weakly as he lay the machine gun on the ground.

"Kick the gun over here," Calico ordered.

"No, Luke. Don't do it," I yelled, struggling to free myself from Calico's grip.

Luke ignored me and pushed the gun toward us with his foot. I couldn't believe he did it, actually gave Calico the gun. We were going to die for sure.

"You sucka-ass, pussy-whooped-ass nigga. Big Chief would be disappointed to see this shit. No way he would die over a bitch. Y'all gotta have different fathers," Calico said as he threw me to the floor and picked up the gun. "I'm not gon' shoot yo' ass like you did my boys, Luke. You and these two bitches gon' die slow," Calico said, pulling the clip from the gun and dislodging the bullet from the chamber.

After the rifle was empty, he tossed all the parts aside and walked toward Luke with his knife high in the air. Luke put up his dukes. "I'ma do what Money and Buck was supposed to do," Calico sneered.

I thought I seen Luke smile. "You gone die just like Buck, Calico."

Calico let out an unimpressed smirk before lunging at Luke, the knife aiming for his throat. He was barely able to dodge the attack.

"Don't run from me, nigga. Don't be a pussy," Calico teased.

"Put that knife down and I'll show you a pussy."

Calico lunged again, swinging the knife in arcing motions. Luke backpedaled, dodging his attacks. While they fought, I began trying to get the rope from my wrists. Since my arms were behind my back, I had to go on feeling alone.

"How the fuck you get out anyway, nigga? I thought yo' ass was gon' die in prison just like yo' brother."

"Appeal."

"That shit works, huh? Too bad. You should've stayed in. You would've lived longer," Calico said before charging Luke again.

Luke couldn't dodge the knife this time. Instead, he used both hands to grab Calico's wrist and block the attack. Calico reacted quickly, using his free hand to punch him in the face. When Luke stumbled backward and let go of the knife, Calico slashed him across the chest.

"Ah, shit!" Luke screamed, grabbing at his wound.

"Oh yeah! Shit burns, huh?" Calico smiled. When he lunged again, Luke was ready. He side-stepped Calico's attack and landed a couple punches to his face. Calico absorbed the punches and swung the knife again, cutting Luke across the stomach.

"Ah, fuck!"

"I see yo' bitch-ass can fight, huh?" Calico asked, rubbing his jaw.

Luke looked like he was getting weak. His shirt was cut up and covered in blood, and he kept one hand across his stomach wound. When he looked toward the machine gun, Calico lunged at him again. Luke used both hands to grab his wrist. Calico took advantage of Luke's failing strength and head-butted him in the face. Luke stumbled, but never let go of his wrist.

I ignored the pain shooting up and down my leg as I worked the ropes on my wrists. If I didn't get free soon, Calico was going to kill my man.

"Mom!" Trinity whispered.

I looked away from the fight and seen Trinity watching me. Blood covered her face and most of her upper body, but she was alive. I was still pissed at her betrayal, but I pushed it to the back of my mind. I needed her help.

"Come untie me."

"My chest hurts. I don't think I can move."

I had no sympathy. "Get up and untie me!"

She moved slowly, scooting over to me when my attention was drawn back to Luke and Calico. They had fallen on the floor, Calico on top. He gained leverage over Luke quickly, sitting on top of him and pushing the knife toward Luke's throat. He tried to keep the knife away, but from my spot on the floor it looked like he was losing. The point of the knife inched slowly toward Luke's throat. Calico wore a victorious smile.

That's when I felt Trinity's hands tugging at the ropes on my wrist. When I was free, I crawled to my feet and limped toward the assault rifle. The clip was only a couple feet away.

Calico's body stiffened when I reloaded the gun. He turned to look at me as I took aim. I was less than twenty feet away. I could see the fear flash in his eyes as I squeezed the trigger.

I fired three shots. All of the bullets hit home, one of them opening a crater in his head. He fell on top of Luke, dead.

"Are you okay, baby?" I asked, limping over to them.

"Urgh! Yeah!" he grunted, tossing Calico's lifeless body aside.

"Why the fuck did you give him the gun?" I snapped.

"I couldn't let him hurt you, baby. Where the fuck did you learn to shoot like that?"

"Practice. Don't you ever give our enemy the gun! Ever!"

"We good, baby. You got him. You saved us."

When I looked toward Calico's lifeless body, a sense of relief rushed through me. Luke stood and reached for the assault rifle. "Give me the gun. Tahiti is outside. She came home right after you left and we tracked your phone. You and Trinity get to the hospital. I'll clean this shit up."

"No!"

"Syn, you gotta go. Y'all bleeding. She got shot."

"She betrayed me, baby."

He looked confused. "What?"

I limped over to Trinity. She was still lying on the ground bleeding. It hurt my heart to see her in pain, but I Ignored it. "How could you do me like that? You betrayed me."

"I'm sorry. I didn't know what to do. He was going to kill me. I didn't want to die," she cried.

"So you almost get us both killed? That shit was stupid! You knew this was dangerous when you got involved. You don't betray the people you love. I did everything for you. I picked you up when you was down. I tried to make up for lost time. I was there for you. I had your back. I loved you."

"I know, Syncere. I'm sorry. I don't want to die. Can't we leave now? It's over."

"C'mon, baby," Luke spoke up. "We have to go. Get out of here and let me clean this up. The police are probably at the house already. I'm going to have to turn myself in. Let me help her get to the car," Luke said, reaching for my daughter.

"Don't touch her!" I yelled, pointing the gun at Trinity.

Luke paused to look at me. "C'mon, baby. Whatever she did, it's all over now. You have to get her to the hospital. She is your daughter. Your flesh and blood. You don't want to do this."

"She betrayed me, Luke. Almost got me killed. I can't forgive her for this. I can't."

"I'm sorry, Mom. Please," Trinity begged.

When I looked down at her, I seen the baby I gave birth to. She was beautiful and precious. I didn't want to cry, but I couldn't stop the tears. Hearing her call me 'Mom' had touched something deep inside of me. She was my flesh and blood. My baby. The only family I had left.

But she betrayed me. I couldn't let it go.

So I pulled the trigger.

J-Blunt

Epilogue

"Who is that hot black chick who keeps eyeing you at the bar?" Larry Heath asked.

Upon hearing that a woman was watching him, Mitchell Sellers looked in the direction Larry had mentioned. He spotted her sitting at the bar: a light-skinned black woman with fiery red hair wearing a tight-fitting red dress. She had large breasts and a butt so big it covered the entire bar stool.

"Man, she's hot," Mitchell muttered.

"You know her?" asked Mitchell's co-worker and longtime friend.

"No. Haven't fucked a black girl since college. And I definitely didn't go to school with her."

When the mystery woman noticed Larry and Mitchell staring, she gave them a flirty wink and wave. They both waved back.

"Really? Since college? Where the fuck have you been? Outer space?" Larry asked as he sipped from his bottle of Bud Light and continued to ogle the woman.

Larry was a 36-year-old blonde-haired bachelor. He was handsome in a rugged cowboy sort of way. Normally, when he was out with Mitchell, the girls hit on him. But not today. Today, Mitchell had the action.

"It's called marriage, moron. I have been with Marcy for almost twenty years. Remember?" Mitchell said sarcastically.

"I know one thing. Marcy doesn't have tits like that. Not that I was looking, of course."

"Yeah, well, I'm not a big fan of the jungle fever thing. It was cool back in college, but—"

"Jungle fever? You fucking kidding me? This ain't 1984. Why do you think Bill Moyers had Karrine Steffans? Why Robin Thicke had Paula Patton? Why those two dumbasses were fighting over Halle Berry?"

Mitchell stared at him, awaiting an answer.

"Because black chicks are fucking nymphos! Want it all the time, any time. Look at those lips, Mitch. They were made for sucking cocks."

"You're crazy, pal," Mitchell laughed.

"No, you're crazy for not getting your ass up from this table and going over to talk to her."

"It probably isn't what you think, man. You're always thinking with your dick."

"Mitch, she's in a fucking pub. Alone. How many black chicks come in here alone? None! She's out for some fun, man. You have to go over there. You're 45 years old, slightly chubby, and severely overworked. You need to take a ride on the wild side. C'mon, man. Quit being such a fucking wuss. Live a little."

Mitchell became silent. It had been a while since he took a ride on the wild side. Shit, as he sat and thought about it, it had been a long time since he'd had sex with his wife. Three weeks and four days, to be exact.

"Alright, man. I'll go speak to her, jeez. Don't have a fucking cow," Mitchell said as he got up from the table and made his way across the bar to the redhead. "Hey, sweetheart. You from around here?" Mitchell asked as he walked up to the bar.

The woman turned and looked at Mitchell like she wanted to eat him.

"Actually, I'm not. Just in town for the weekend. Do I look that out of place?"

"This is a regular hangout for attorneys and police officers. I've never seen you in a law firm or interrogation room."

"That's because I've been waiting on the right man to come make me confess," she flirted, pulling the tooth-picked olive from her martini glass and running her tongue across it.

Mitchell stood mesmerized and watched her tongue tease the fruit. When he felt a tingle in the front of his pants, he knew he had to sit down.

"Is this seat taken?"

"Only if you want it. Do you want it?" she asked, leaving Mitchell wondering if she was talking about her or the seat.

218

"Yeah. Sure. Absolutely. The name is Mitch. You?"

"Ferrary. Like the car," she smiled, popping the small green ball into her mouth.

Mitchell took the time to look over her body. He had a hard time pulling his eyes away from her chest. Her breasts were huge, and the strapless red dress barely covered her areolas.

"Wow. How appropriate. You have crazy curves. Can I buy you a drink?"

"Sure. A martini. Shaken, not stirred," she joked, quoting the famous spy as she erupted with laughter. When she did so, she placed a hand on his thigh and squeezed.

"Hey, Russ! Martini. Shaken, not stirred," he called to the barkeep. "So, what brings you out tonight, Ferrary?"

"I don't know much about this city, and I was hoping I could find someone to show me a good time. You look big and strong. I like big and strong. Can you show me a good time?" she asked, biting her bottom lip and moving her hand further up his thigh.

Mitchell felt his member rise. "Depends on how you define fun."

"My fun is uninhibited. Are you uninhibited?" Ferrary asked, running her hand across his hardening penis.

"Uninhibited is my middle name," Mitchell smiled.

"I have a hotel room around the corner. Wanna cum?" she asked, her voice dripping sex appeal.

"Uh, Ross! On second thought, hold that drink!"

***

"Ooh! Look at this big dick. I love sucking big dicks!" Ferrary moaned as she knelt between Mitchell's legs.

"Oh, God! This is so fucking hot!" Mitchell beamed.

They were back in her hotel room, on the bed, both of them naked. She was jacking him off and sucking his balls. Mitchell watched with wide eyes as Ferrary did things to him that his wife refused to do. He was so happy he took Larry's advice. Her lips were just like he said: made for sucking cock. And when she wrapped those juicy lips around his pole, he sucked in air as if he was drowning. Ferrary deep throated all five inches of him, fondling his balls as she chewed him. When he was on the verge of cumming, Ferrary stopped sucking him and began jacking him off.

"Oh, fuck! Yeah!" he groaned as he came in her hand.

"Aw, no fair," Ferrary whined as Mitchell's penis deflated.

"Wait. I just need a few minutes. I have an idea. Stay like this," Mitchell said, keeping her on all fours as he crawled behind her. "Wow. You have a great ass."

"Track and field. I– Ooh!" Ferrary moaned when she felt Mitchell's tongue lick her ass crack. This was new to her. It felt so good that it brought tears to her eyes. And just when she didn't think it could get any better, it did. He spread her cheeks and stuck his tongue into her anus, pumping it in and out like a dildo.

"Oh, shit! Ah! Oh!" Ferrary moaned.

When she came, her orgasm felt so good she cried a little bit. "Damn, Mitch. That shit was hot!" Ferrary said as she fell onto the bed. That's when she noticed the red head of his erect penis. "Ooh. You're back!"

"Yeah. Mind getting back on your knees again?" he asked, stroking himself.

"Ooh! I love doggy style."

When Mitchell entered her from behind, Ferrary screamed like he was packing twelve inches. "Oh yeah, Mitch! You're so big! Let me know when you're about to cum. I want you to cum on my titties."

It didn't take long for Mitchell's second orgasm to bubble up. "I'm about to make it!" he groaned.

Ferrary spun around and began jacking him off. When he came, she used to head of his penis to smear his semen over her breasts.

"Are you still uninhibited?" Ferrary asked as she continued to stroke his softening penis.

"What did you have in mind?"

"Clean them off," she said, looking down at her shiny, sperm-coated breasts.

Mitchell looked taken aback. He never imagined eating his own semen. Then again, he knew he would probably never experience another night like this again. "Well, why the hell not? It's my cum." With that, he bent down and began tasting his own body fluid, licking her breasts like they were ice cream cones.

"Ooh, Mitch! You are such a freak!" Ferrary moaned.

Mitchell was having the time of his life licking Ferrary's breasts clean until he was interrupted. The closet door opened, and out walked a light-skinned black woman wearing a black leather cat suit. Mitchell immediately thought threesome.

"You are a nasty motherfucker!" the woman hissed.

Mitchell's thoughts of a ménage immediately vanished. "Who the fuck are you? What do you want? What is going on?" Mitchell asked, looking scared. He knew he'd seen the woman before, but he wasn't sure where. But that was the least of his problems. The biggest problem was the tablet she held in her hands.

"Last week you locked up my man. Unless you want your wife and the rest of the world to see you eat shit and your own cum, I suggest you not re-try Luke Swanson and give him self-defense."

Mitchell's mouth fell open. He was in deep shit literally and figuratively. *Let Swanson to free?* The mere thought of it made in sick on the stomach. He had to think fast. At the moment, no solution was too wild to consider. Not when his entire career was on the line.

The thoughts that ran to his mind were just as criminal as anything Luke had done. Mitchell had no choice but to shot or get off the toilet. And it was in that very second, he decided his fate...

To Be Continued...
A Gangster's Syn 3
Coming Soon

Submission Guideline

Submit the first three chapters of your completed manuscript to ldpsubmissions@gmail.com, subject line: Your book's title. The manuscript must be in a .doc file and sent as an attachment. Document should be in Times New Roman, double spaced and in size 12 font. Also, provide your synopsis and full contact information. If sending multiple submissions, they must each be in a separate email.

Have a story but no way to send it electronically? You can still submit to LDP/Ca$h Presents. Send in the first three chapters, written or typed, of your completed manuscript to:

LDP: Submissions Dept
Po Box 870494
Mesquite, Tx 75187

DO NOT send original manuscript. Must be a duplicate.

Provide your synopsis and a cover letter containing your full contact information.

Thanks for considering LDP and Ca$h Presents.

A Gangster's Syn 2

Coming Soon from Lock Down Publications/Ca$h Presents

BOW DOWN TO MY GANGSTA
By **Ca$h**
TORN BETWEEN TWO
By **Coffee**
BLOOD STAINS OF A SHOTTA **III**
By **Jamaica**
STEADY MOBBIN **III**
By **Marcellus Allen**
RENEGADE BOYS IV
By Meesha
BLOOD OF A BOSS **VI**
SHADOWS OF THE GAME II
By **Askari**
LOYAL TO THE GAME **IV**
LIFE OF SIN **III**
By **T.J. & Jelissa**
A DOPEBOY'S PRAYER **II**
By **Eddie "Wolf" Lee**
IF LOVING YOU IS WRONG… **III**
By **Jelissa**
TRUE SAVAGE **VII**
By **Chris Green**
BLAST FOR ME **III**
DUFFLE BAG CARTEL **IV**
HEARTLESS GOON **II**
By **Ghost**
A HUSTLER'S DECEIT III
KILL ZONE **II**

J-Blunt

BAE BELONGS TO ME III

SOUL OF A MONSTER II

By **Aryanna**

THE COST OF LOYALTY **III**

By **Kweli**

A GANGSTER'S SYN III

By **J-Blunt**

KING OF NEW YORK V

RISE TO POWER III

COKE KINGS III

By **T.J. Edwards**

GORILLAZ IN THE BAY IV

De'Kari

THE STREETS ARE CALLING II

Duquie Wilson

KINGPIN KILLAZ IV

STREET KINGS III

PAID IN BLOOD II

Hood Rich

SINS OF A HUSTLA II

ASAD

TRIGGADALE III

Elijah R. Freeman

MARRIED TO A BOSS III

By Destiny Skai & Chris Green

KINGZ OF THE GAME IV

Playa Ray

SLAUGHTER GANG III

RUTHLESS HEART

By Willie Slaughter

A Gangster's Syn 2

THE HEART OF A SAVAGE II

By Jibril Williams

FUK SHYT II

By Blakk Diamond

THE DOPEMAN'S BODYGAURD II

By Tranay Adams

TRAP GOD

By Troublesome

YAYO

By S. Allen

GHOST MOB

Stilloan Robinson

KINGPIN DREAMS

By Paper Boi Rari

CREAM

By Yolanda Moore

<u>**Available Now**</u>

<u>RESTRAINING ORDER **I & II**</u>

By **CA$H & Coffee**

<u>LOVE KNOWS NO BOUNDARIES **I II & III**</u>

By **Coffee**

<u>RAISED AS A GOON I, II, III & IV</u>

<u>BRED BY THE SLUMS I, II, III</u>

<u>BLAST FOR ME I & II</u>

<u>ROTTEN TO THE CORE I II III</u>

<u>A BRONX TALE I, II, III</u>

J-Blunt

A Gangster's Syn 2

A GANGSTER'S CODE I &, II III

A GANGSTER'S SYN II

By J-Blunt

PUSH IT TO THE LIMIT

By **Bre' Hayes**

BLOOD OF A BOSS **I, II, III, IV, V**

SHADOWS OF THE GAME

By **Askari**

THE STREETS BLEED MURDER **I, II & III**

THE HEART OF A GANGSTA I II& III

By **Jerry Jackson**

CUM FOR ME

CUM FOR ME 2

CUM FOR ME 3

CUM FOR ME 4

CUM FOR ME 5

An **LDP Erotica Collaboration**

BRIDE OF A HUSTLA **I II & II**

THE FETTI GIRLS **I, II& III**

CORRUPTED BY A GANGSTA I, II III, IV

BLINDED BY HIS LOVE

By **Destiny Skai**

WHEN A GOOD GIRL GOES BAD

By **Adrienne**

THE COST OF LOYALTY I II

By Kweli

A GANGSTER'S REVENGE **I II III & IV**

THE BOSS MAN'S DAUGHTERS

THE BOSS MAN'S DAUGHTERS II

THE BOSSMAN'S DAUGHTERS III

J-Blunt

THE BOSSMAN'S DAUGHTERS IV

THE BOSS MAN'S DAUGHTERS **V**

A SAVAGE LOVE **I & II**

BAE BELONGS TO ME I II

A HUSTLER'S DECEIT I, II, III

WHAT BAD BITCHES DO I, II, III

SOUL OF A MONSTER

KILL ZONE

By **Aryanna**

A KINGPIN'S AMBITON

A KINGPIN'S AMBITION **II**

I MURDER FOR THE DOUGH

By **Ambitious**

TRUE SAVAGE

TRUE SAVAGE II

TRUE SAVAGE **III**

TRUE SAVAGE **IV**

TRUE SAVAGE **V**

TRUE SAVAGE **VI**

By **Chris Green**

A DOPEBOY'S PRAYER

By **Eddie "Wolf" Lee**

THE KING CARTEL **I, II & III**

By **Frank Gresham**

THESE NIGGAS AIN'T LOYAL **I, II & III**

By **Nikki Tee**

GANGSTA SHYT **I II &III**

By **CATO**

THE ULTIMATE BETRAYAL

By **Phoenix**

BOSS'N UP **I , II & III**

By **Royal Nicole**

I LOVE YOU TO DEATH

By Destiny J

I RIDE FOR MY HITTA

I STILL RIDE FOR MY HITTA

By **Misty Holt**

LOVE & CHASIN' PAPER

By **Qay Crockett**

TO DIE IN VAIN

SINS OF A HUSTLA

By **ASAD**

BROOKLYN HUSTLAZ

By **Boogsy Morina**

BROOKLYN ON LOCK I & II

By **Sonovia**

GANGSTA CITY

By **Teddy Duke**

A DRUG KING AND HIS DIAMOND I & II III

A DOPEMAN'S RICHES

HER MAN, MINE'S TOO I, II

CASH MONEY HO'S

By Nicole Goosby

TRAPHOUSE KING **I II & III**

KINGPIN KILLAZ I II III

STREET KINGS I II

PAID IN BLOOD

By **Hood Rich**

LIPSTICK KILLAH **I, II, III**

CRIME OF PASSION I & II

J-Blunt

By **Mimi**

STEADY MOBBN' **I, II, III**

By **Marcellus Allen**

WHO SHOT YA **I, II, III**

Renta

GORILLAZ IN THE BAY **I II III**

DE'KARI

TRIGGADALE I II

Elijah R. Freeman

GOD BLESS THE TRAPPERS I, II, III

THESE SCANDALOUS STREETS I, II, III

FEAR MY GANGSTA I, II, III

THESE STREETS DON'T LOVE NOBODY I, II

BURY ME A G I, II, III, IV, V

A GANGSTA'S EMPIRE I, II, III, IV

THE DOPEMAN'S BODYGAURD

Tranay Adams

THE STREETS ARE CALLING

Duquie Wilson

MARRIED TO A BOSS… I II

By Destiny Skai & Chris Green

KINGZ OF THE GAME I II III

Playa Ray

SLAUGHTER GANG I II

By Willie Slaughter

THE HEART OF A SAVAGE

By Jibril Williams

FUK SHYT

By Blakk Diamond

DON'T F#CK WITH MY HEART I II

230

A Gangster's Syn 2

By Linnea

ADDICTED TO THE DRAMA I II III

By Jamila

BOOKS BY LDP'S CEO, CA$H

TRUST IN NO MAN

TRUST IN NO MAN 2

TRUST IN NO MAN 3

BONDED BY BLOOD

SHORTY GOT A THUG

THUGS CRY

THUGS CRY 2

THUGS CRY 3

TRUST NO BITCH

TRUST NO BITCH 2

TRUST NO BITCH 3

TIL MY CASKET DROPS

RESTRAINING ORDER

RESTRAINING ORDER 2

IN LOVE WITH A CONVICT

Coming Soon

BONDED BY BLOOD 2

BOW DOWN TO MY GANGSTA

A Gangster's Syn 2